I0619004

Shadow Ascending

Children of the Goddess, Volume 7

Prudence MacLeod

Published by Prudence MacLeod, 2024.

Shadow Ascending
by
Prudence MacLeod
Copyright Jan. 04/2018
Book seven in the Children of the Goddess Series
Forewarned

This is a work of fiction. Similarities to real people, places, or events are entirely coincidental.

SHADOW ASCENDING

First edition. January 16, 2024.

Written by Prudence MacLeod.

After the battle of the fishmen, the daughters of Moragah had a time of peace, a time to rest and heal. Eventually each returned to their lives as they had known them before that battle occurred. Still, Lady Shadow was disturbed, for she and she alone could feel the unease of their goddess.

Time passed, and that unease grew. The Watcher rarely came down from her tower, and then it was for a quick meal before she returned. One day Shadow followed her back to the sanctuary of the tower. "Lady Watcher, I can feel your distress, what is it that disturbs you so?"

"I can't see it. I know it's there, but I can't see it."

"Explain."

"There's something, something dark and evil growing, especially in certain nearby places. It's close, but not in, North Bay, Georgia City, Lenora's ... I can't be sure, but something is out there, and it looks like it's gearing up to attack us, all at once. There's even one building up out west, near where the Chosen have their headquarters."

"And you have no idea what it is?"

"None. The whole damn thing is so cloudy, but it's scaring me and ..." just then her phone buzzed, and she glanced down. "It's Justice." She put the phone on speaker as she answered. "Watcher here."

"Miranda, It's Tasha. Girl, Allie is here and wants to know why there's such a big military build up just outside of town. You got anything on that?"

"Justice, this is Shadow. Miranda is in trance ..."

"Oh fuck."

"Miranda?"

"Tasha, hide your people. They're coming in heavy and fast."

Before she finished speaking Shadow was gone from the room, hurrying down the stairs. Suddenly the presence of Moragah engulfed her. *"Seline, there is no more time. They're coming, and all will perish. You're the only hope for the priestesses to survive. Stop holding back and embrace what you are. Get them out."*

1

As suddenly as she had come, Moragah was gone, and Miranda was calling frantically as she raced down the stairs. She found Shadow halfway down. Lady Shadow, shaken to the core, swallowed hard then locked her gaze on Miranda. "Get all our people to the mansion, quickly. Warn Lenora to spirit her people away from that town, I will find them. Go."

With that Shadow vanished and Miranda continued her swift descent of the stairs, calling for Ellen.

ON A LONELY AND WINDSWEPT planet, devoid of animate life, Lady Shadow stood breathing deeply, fighting for control of her emotions. Finally, she squared her shoulders, a snarl on her perfect lips. "I must release my hold on my darker nature and be all I can be? Fine then. So be it." She vanished from there to appear in the sewers of Lady Justice's home.

Beneath the streets of Georgia City all looked like chaos. A man in uniform was bellowing orders and soldiers were assembling. Other people were hurrying down a rough path from the streets. Lady Shadow stepped from the darkened corner and strode toward the man in charge. "Intel, are they all here?"

"Still coming, Lady Shadow. What's happening?"

"Military. They're coming in heavy." She waved her arm and a glowing transparent disk of light appeared beside her. "Send your people through this portal, quickly as possible. Rest and await me on the other side."

He turned and began bawling orders. Men and women in uniform swiftly began moving through the portal and disappearing. Shadow stood beside the glowing disc, urging them on to greater speed. In mere moments they were all through. "Intel, are there more?"

"We have guards out on the streets, and friends from the city coming. Are they welcome?"

"They are vital. Do what you can to speed them up. Where are Kara and Tasha?"

"Bringing the civilians of the inner circle."

Even as he spoke the first shell exploded above. "Dammit," snarled Shadow. "Intel, guard the portal. Nothing unfriendly is to pass through." With that she ran for the surface. Two more shells exploded before the armored priestess reached the street.

She swept her arms wide and the falling shells began to explode in the air. Debris fell against the unseen dome as Shadow stood like an angry god amid the madness. Two armored warriors herded human civilians toward her as she held the attacking mortar fire at bay.

"Lady Shadow."

"Down below, Justice. There's a portal. Get your people through it quickly as possible. Go!"

"This way, hurry," shouted the warrior with the scales of justice emblazoned on her armor. She scooped one woman into her arms and carried her away.

A smaller warrior appeared at Shadow's side. "How can I help?"

"Below. Get Intel and the others through the portal. Kara, is that all of your people?"

"All we can get to."

"When all have passed through the portal return to me."

With a nod the tiny warrior fled toward the sewers. She was back within moments. "Clear."

"Then through the portal with you, swiftly now." As the warrior fled to the portal, Lady Shadow counted to ten then dropped her arms and the unseen dome vanished. As debris fell around her and armed soldiers charged forward, she vanished from sight.

On an empty planet dozens of people gathered together, guarded by the Soldiers of Justice. Kara appeared then the portal dissolved behind her. A moment later Lady Shadow stepped from the shade beside a boulder. "Intel."

"Lady Shadow, what happened?"

"They came at you with a full military attack. We were unaware of this piece of treachery until the last moment. Take your people to that building in the distance. A man will meet you there. He will assist you in many ways. Intel, he's not human, but do not fear him, he's here to help.

"Justice, Kara, with me." They came to her and took her hands. All three vanished to reappear high on a rooftop in Georgia city. "Now, quickly, who is missing and where do we find them?"

"Just Jess, the chief of police, and Bill Murdock," replied Lady Justice. "They were at work when the world went all to hell. Jess called with a warning, but it was nearly too late. She'll be at the police station, so will Bill and the chief."

"Then let us fetch them. Place your hand on my shoulder and think of Jessica." As Tasha's hand touched her shoulder, a visual of Jessica appeared in her mind.

JESSICA LOGAN SCHOOLED her face as the big man in uniform continued to berate her as a traitor. She was in restraints and being interrogated. Suddenly something moved in the shadows. The uniform gulped and jumped back as Lady Shadow stepped into the room, seized Jessica Logan in her arms then vanished. A few moments later Bill Murdock was pulled into the ether from his desk. The chief soon followed.

"Through the portal now, quickly."

"What about you?" asked Lady Justice.

"I have more of our people to find. Join the others and I'll meet you there as soon as I can. Go, Tasha, see to your folk." They stepped through the portal then it vanished. Lady Shadow retreated into the shadows as a squad of heavily armed soldiers burst onto the rooftop.

INTEL STOOD WHERE LADY Shadow had been but a moment before, collecting his thoughts. With a sigh, he squared his shoulders and turned to face the assembled people. They were confused, frightened, and they looked to him to take charge since Lady Shadow had vanished once again.

"All right, people, listen up. The Soldiers of Justice, and their allies, were attacked by the military forces of our own country. They came at us with mortar and shell fire, into an area heavily populated by civilians. Lady Shadow brought us out in time.

"The Lady told me to approach those buildings. She said a man would meet us there, that he will help us. So, make yourselves comfortable. Finder, assign a detail to protect these people. Blockade, you're with me. We'll go talk to this guy and see what he can do for us."

The soldiers swiftly formed a defensive circle around the civilians. Intel and Blockade headed toward the buildings. As they approached, a figure appeared from an arched doorway and came to meet them.

The creature was humanoid, but taller with green scaled skin, small tight fitted ears, long arms ending in three fingered hands. His face was lean with deep set amber eyes, and a slightly jutting lower jaw with short tusks. Hairless except for a single stripe of bristly dark hair running down the middle of his head, he was an imposing sight.

As he neared his visitors he spoke, but it all came out in gibberish. With a half snarl and a muttered curse, he batted at something attached to his tunic. It sputtered a few times then he tried again. "Welcome to Eelion, I greet you in the name of Lady Shadow. I am Gornagsh Egrath Deximth Extondra Alion. Call me Dex."

Intel grinned as he offered his hand. "I'm Staff Sergeant Fredrick Johnathon Eccles deceased. Call me Intel." The creature grinned his delight as he gripped Intel's hand then released him. "This man is Blockade."

"Hey Dex, call me Block."

They shook hands then Dex spoke again. "Did I get the handshake thing right?"

"You did," replied Blockade.

"Excellent. Lady Shadow taught me. She also told me to assist you in any way I can. Tell me what you need."

"Information first," replied Intel. "Where are we?"

"Eelion."

"Okay, so, not Earth."

"No, far away from, in a parallel universe. Lady Shadow has been here many times before. She once said she might send people here to be kept safe. She told me to help wherever possible, so, here we are." A great sadness came over him and his broad shoulders slumped. "Eelion is a place of the dead now, nothing left but things and memories."

"What happened here?" asked Blockade.

"Long ago, Eelion pulsed with life, forests, oceans, millions of species, billions of people. As the populations grew, different factions began to fight for the remaining resources. The death toll on all sides was terrible.

"A group of scientists invented a powerful weapon, a doomsday weapon. A weapon so destructive no one would ever dare to use it, and they gave it to all opposing factions, believing that the threat would force the wars to end. It didn't. Instead the fools used the weapon. It destroyed all animate life. Over time even the corpses and skeletons returned to dust.

"That time was eons ago."

"So, how do you know all this?" asked Intel.

"I was the leader of the team that invented the weapon. As the dissolution came devouring everything, I tried to kill myself, but Lady Shadow appeared riding on her dragon and brought me through time to here, to the now.

"She made me the guardian of this place. From time to time she needs things, and I provide what I can. The rest of the time I try to reconstruct the history and art of my people. I hope to leave something more than this destruction of them for future explorers to find."

Intel nodded. He couldn't imagine the torment this creature lived with. "Okay. Look, Dex, Shadow brought us here, saved us from certain death, but I have no idea at all what she has planned for us. Right now, I need food, water, and shelter for my people. Can you help us with this?"

"I can. This place was once a military base. Come, I will show you to the barracks." He turned and led them toward a building. He stopped a short distance from it, held up some sort of remote, there was a shimmer in the air, then he led them onward.

Inside they found a massive barracks, spotlessly clean and ready for use. "The plumbing and drinking water are all functional," said Dex as he showed them around. "Through that archway is/was the food preparation and eating area, but there are few supplies ready. The machines are still working on that.

"Lady Shadow brought me here and told me to prepare the place in case she needed it. I cleaned it up, made everything functional, but I have gathered little food, not knowing if anyone would ever come. Until today, she has only accessed a few suits of battle armor."

"So this is where she gets the armor," rumbled Blockade. "We could sure use some of that."

"The storehouse is full of werj fnier tanf weoir we ..." With a muttered curse Dex batted at the object on his tunic making it hiss again. "I really need to pick up a new one of these. As I was saying, there is armor in plenty. If the lady wishes it so, I will provide you will all you need."

"We'll set that to the back burner for now," said Intel. "Right now, I want to get my people in out of the sun."

"Then bring them here," said Dex. "Fetch them and I'll get the power up. I will then start up the food processors. It will take some time, but before the sun retires for the day there will be food."

Intel nodded and reached for the comm at his shoulder. "Finder, bring them in." No response, so he tried again. "Finder, are you there?"

"Is that a communication device?"

"Yes."

"Just a moment." Dex went to a panel on the wall, touched something that made the whole wall shimmer momentarily. "Try it now."

"Intel to Finder. Do you read?"

"Loud and clear, Sir."

"Bring the people here. Blockade will meet you to show you the way."

"Roger that. Coming in."

A short time later Finder and Blockade led them into the barracks. Intel was organizing them, assigning bunks and jobs, when Shadow appeared with Little Blue, Lady Justice, Jessica Logan, the chief of police, and Bill Murdock. "Intel, all is well here?"

"All under control here, Lady Shadow."

"Then I leave you to it. Dex, will this barracks hold this many more?"

"Ten times this number easily, Great Lady," he replied as he knelt at her feet.

"Is there another close by?"

"There is. Will we need it?"

"We will. There is another group, somewhat less disciplined than these folks. I think it best to give them their own space."

"I will prepare for their arrival, Great Lady." He rose from where he'd knelt as she vanished. "You do not kneel before the goddess?"

"She's not a goddess," said Tasha. "She's our leader, but we all serve Moragah, Goddess of Wisdom, Defender of the Weak."

"You are the woman who deals out justice, yes? She has told me of this Moragah, but my mind cannot encompass that, nor have I ever sensed that presence, but I have seen the power of Lady Shadow. I have felt the strength of this goddess, and I believe She knows not Her full reach Herself. It is She I serve."

"Fair enough," grinned Kara, winking Tasha. "She gave you an order, better hop to it." He gave her a quick bow then hurried away.

"So, Lady J, what now?" asked Intel as he approached.

"Now we check to see if we have all our people, then we settle in and wait for Seline. Something tells me we weren't the only ones hit. I'm betting we get company and lots of it soon."

"Okay, then I'll start prepping for their arrival."

Retreat

Miranda raced into the living room, shouting for Ellen who swiftly appeared from another room. "Miranda, slow down. What is it?"

"Military. They're coming for us and using heavy weapons."

"Heavy weapons?"

"Artillery, tanks, hundreds of troops. We have to get everyone here to the mansion."

Ellen whipped out her phone and called. She found Decoy chatting with Lady Blue and the Warrior. "Decoy, you've got incoming. Artillery, tanks, and ground troops. Get everyone here to the mansion. Come through the sewers, get as close as you can before you expose yourself."

"Understood Ellen." He leaped to his feet and started bawling orders.

"Penny, Vic and Jack are out on patrol. You stay here and help Decoy, I'll search for Vic."

"They were headed for the waterfront, Warrior," replied Lady Blue. "Go."

Within moments nearly fifty soldiers and a few civilians were moving swiftly through the sewers. They were barely away from their headquarters when the first shell burst through the pavement. A rain of hellfire descended on the area they were known to protect, but they were no longer there. As they moved beneath the streets, they heard the heavy vehicles rumble by overhead.

"Pick it up, people," shouted Decoy. "They'll be after us any minute."

"Keep them going, Decoy," shouted Penny. "I'll drop back and slow the enemy down as best I can." He hurried onward, silently thanking Moragah that he'd made them explore and map every bit of storm sewer they could access.

"Gas! They're pumping gas into the sewers," came a shout from the rear of the column.

"Get topside, now," roared Decoy as he spotted a ladder and raced to it. He climbed it and gave a mighty heave against the lid. It moved out of the way, but he saw the troops moving in. Decoy scrambles out of the man hole, took shelter, then opened fire, providing cover for his people emerging from the sewers.

The soldiers of Justice climbed swiftly to the street then joined Decoy in laying down covering fire. Suddenly Lady Blue was there in full battle armor, helping the civilian out of the way and to shelter. The last one scurried behind a building and Penny hurried to the soldiers. "Decoy?"

"Here. Running low on ammo."

"Get them moving, I'll slow these guys down."

To the horror of the attacking soldiers, the armored figure ran straight at them, their bullets bouncing off her. She tore into them like a hurricane, hurling bodies in all directions, her guns dropping man after man.

As her guns ran empty she switched to her knives with deadly effect, until a grenade exploded against her chest, knocking her back off balance. Three men leaped on her but were suddenly ripped away. The warrior had joined the fight. As Lady Blue regained her feet she saw the enemy reinforcements arriving.

The new troops leaped from the trucks to join the battle, but an engine screamed and a big black car ploughed through them. Something exploded, and the car was thrown through the air to land heavily on its side then topple to the ground on blown wheels.

Jack Longtree groaned and cut the seatbelt free. "Hey, Viper, we having fun yet?"

"Getting there. You functional?"

"Think so. We should move."

"Roger that."

The car door was suddenly torn away by Lady Blue. "You guys okay?"

"Somewhat," growled Viper as he crawled from the destroyed car and struggled to his feet.

Penny was helping Jack from the car. "Okay, guys, Decoy and troops went that way, they've got a way to go, but they're headed for the mansion. Join up and do what you can to help them, Lacy and I'll try to keep these troops off you."

The two armored warriors moved off to join Decoy and his soldiers while Lady Blue joined the Lady Warrior. She arrived in the fight just as Lacy got hit with rocket fire. She staggered back but didn't fall. As Penny tore the weapon from the soldier's hands, Lady Warrior rejoined the battle. "Lacy, we need to fall back. There's just too damn many of them."

"Aw come on, we can take 'em."

"Maybe, but we need to be protecting Decoy's retreat. Come on."

They caught up to their people two blocks from the gates. The soldiers were running out of ammo, but Jack Longtree and the Viper were taking up the slack in their armor. Lady Blue and the Warrior hit their opposition from behind and tore into them. Lacy put them down while Penny salvaged weapons and ammunition.

One block to go and they saw it, a tank flanked by two armored personnel carriers. The warriors in magic armor raced to face this new threat then stopped. Over the chatter of gunfire, they heard the dragon scream his challenge. "Incoming dragon," shouted Lacy as she and Penny turned to help shield their people.

The tank tried desperately to train its main gun on the monstrous beast descending from above. To the driver's horror the dragon rolled aside, and the shell passed harmlessly by. Suddenly the beast spat hellfire and the mighty tank actually began to melt down, as did the two armored personnel carriers beside it did. The soldiers on the ground poured weapon's fire at the dragon and rider, but they ignored it, and then the second dragon screamed. A single pass left only melted metal and charred bodies.

At a gesture from the original dragon rider, the second turned her steed away. The warplane came screaming in, the missile leaped ahead, but the dragon and rider ignored it. A gout of flame from the beast and the missile exploded well out in front of them. The plane came around for another run, but a shining disc appeared in the air and the dragon disappeared through it. The disc disappeared behind the beast.

Back on the ground Decoy and his charges arrived at the gate to the mansion grounds. Lady Shadow appeared, and the gate turned into a shining disc. "Through the portal, swiftly now." They began to file through, carrying their wounded with them. Jack Longtree and Viper were the last to make their escape, then the portal disappeared.

"Sisters, to the mansion. Hurry." They shifted onto combat mode and raced away, Lady Shadow being the last to arrive. She swiftly created another glowing disc. "Miranda, send Ellith back now. Ellen, Debbie, quickly, through the portal. Lady Blue, you and the Watcher as well. Justice will meet you on the other side. Warrior, with me."

As they stepped through the glowing disc and it disappeared behind them, Lady Shadow leaped aboard the dragon's back, the Warrior right behind her. Aeroth leaped into the air. A few beats of mighty wings and they saw the soldiers pouring through the gates.

The dragon roared a challenge then plunged toward the ground, spitting hellfire before him. To the soldier's great surprise, the fire wasn't meant for them, but created some sort of barrier before them. When they finally managed to get around it, they found only an empty lot and a burned-out foundation where a mansion once stood.

Three helicopters raced toward the great beast, but it vanished into a glowing disc. Moragah's children had abandoned North Bay.

LADY SHADOW AND THE Warrior sat aboard the dragon gazing at the burned-out shell of a small house. "Shadow? Do you think they got out in time?"

"The camper is missing, Seeker has eluded them."

"Lenora's going to be pissed they burned her house."

"Truly she is. However, there's no enemy near for us to fight, and no sign of the Seeker. Suggestions?"

Lacy sighed and let her shoulders slump. "I got nothing. You know Lenni, she's as elusive as a breeze. Shadow ..."

"So, you cannot contact Moragah either?"

"No, and I'll readily admit this has me completely freaked out."

"Yes, and me as well."

"Do you know what happened?"

"No. This morning Miranda was distressed, and I went to speak with her. Moragah gave me a warning then vanished."

Moragah suddenly engulfed them. *"Lenora is besieged. Go there."* She was gone in an instant.

Lady Shadow shook herself. "Aeroth, you saw? Go."

The beast leaped into the air, bellowing his challenge. The land sped by below them then they saw a lone warrior in shining armor running a zig-zag pattern, avoiding the gunfire from the pursuing helicopter. With another scream of challenge, the great beast folded his wings and stooped.

Too late the men aboard the chopper saw the gigantic form falling toward them. The helicopter's rotor blades shattered against the dragon's claws and the machine plunged toward the ground. The armored warrior fleeing from the soldiers glanced over her shoulder then raised her arm high. As the dragon banked above her she leaped into the air. Lacy, clinging to the dragon's spinal ridge, leaned down and grasped Lenora's hand, pulling her up onto the beast's back. "Hey there, pretty girl, did you miss me?"

"Shut up, Lacy. Shut up or I'll tell Miranda."

"Lenora, your people, where are they?"

"Behind enemy lines, in the camper. I hid it on a side road then led the soldiers away."

"I'll find them." She created a shining disc in the air before them. "Aeroth, take them to Justice." With that she leaped from his back and plummeted toward the ground while the dragon passed through the portal and vanished.

Shadow plunged downward, her armor glittering in the afternoon sun. As she neared the ground, something huge arose from the shadows of the forest, reaching up to catch her gently and lower her safely to the ground.

The soldiers turned their weapons on her, but she ignored them. A small rocket slammed into her from behind causing her to stagger forward. With a snarl she turned and thrust out her hand. The concussion was terrible, and the soldiers fell to the ground screaming in pain from burst eardrums. The woman in armor vanished into the shadows.

HEATHER JONES SCREAMED as the door of the camper was ripped away. "Heather, Heather, it's Shadow. Come quickly now, come." Heather, Morty, Mary-jo, and Roscoe the dog climbed down to find Lady Shadow standing beside a glowing disc. "Quickly now, through the portal, Lenora will be waiting for you. Go now." She urged Mary-jo and Morty through.

"Heather, tell them I've gone west for the rest of our people." She nodded and followed Morty through the disc, then it vanished. Shadow retreated into trees and was lost to sight.

HEATHER STEPPED THROUGH the portal and leaped into Lenora's arms. "Oh god, Lenni, you're safe. I was terrified for you."

"Hush now, hush sweet Heather. All is well now. Look, there's Roscoe checking the place out and hanging out with Jack. See, everybody's here, safe and sound."

"Lenni, where on Earth is *here*, exactly?"

"That's a bit of a long story. Actually, we're not on Earth anymore. This is a dead world from somewhere, some when. This is where Shadow gets the magic armor from. As I get the story, the people who lived here annihilated themselves eons ago. For now, all that matters, is that we're safe."

"Hi Heather," said Miranda as she approached. "How are you doing? Are you guys all right?"

"Miranda, can you tell me what happened? When you called we ran out, jumped in the camper, gathered up Uncle Morty and Mary-jo then lit out. We passed a military convoy going the other way. Suddenly they turned and came after us. Why? What's going on?"

"I have no idea," sighed Miranda. "I've been watching something build up for weeks, but this morning the buildup was all turning black. Moragah warned Seline to get us out and Lady Shadow brought us here.

"Gods, it was our own military. They hit us all simultaneously, every stronghold of the Priestesses was hit at the same time, trying to wipe us out all at once. Seline didn't come with you?"

"She said to tell you she was going west for the rest of our people, but it looks like everybody is already here."

"She's gone for the Chosen," mused Miranda.

"Who are the Chosen? Wait, that bike gang that terrorizes the entire west coast?" asked Lenora.

"Yes, that's the Chosen. Their leader is a sister we haven't met yet, well, except the Ladies Blue."

"Somebody call me?" grinned Penny as she joined them.

"Lady Watcher says Shadow has gone to bring that bike gang, the Chosen. She said the leader is a sister and you know her?"

"That would be Ryder," sighed Penny. "Guess we'd better warn Dex there's more company coming."

Hard Riders

At the gang's headquarters, several riders were already retreating to the shelter of the big garage. The day was going to be a hot one. As the leader entered one man called out to her. "Hey, Ryder, got your bike all tuned up for you. Purrs like a kitten."

"Thanks, Kyle, you're the best. I ... What is it Thunder? What're you looking at?"

"There," rumbled an impossibly deep voice. "In the shadows."

"Oh fuck, get behind me, everybody."

"Ryder?"

"Get behind me now. Let me deal here."

"What the ..."

"Just do it," she barked as she stepped toward the apparition striding from the shadows. It was a tall woman dressed in gore bespattered armor. The armor vanished to reveal flowing robes. Ryder stepped toward her then dropped to one knee.

"Why do you kneel before me?"

"You're Lady Shadow, Chosen of Moragah, she who leads the sisters of the priesthood. I know who you are, and I know what you are. I pledge to you myself and this motley crew of hard headed riders. What do you need?"

"Accepted. Stand, my sister, Moragah has promised you would never have to kneel again, and I repeat that vow. Stand with me now, shoulder to shoulder as a fellow warrior. Ryder, I need you to gather your people and get on the road, quickly now. They're coming."

"Who's coming?"

"Military, heavy weapons, artillery, armored vehicles, they mean to make an end of the Chosen. They come from the northeast. Ryder, get them out, get them on the road. Go southwest, I'll find you." With a pass of her hand she vanished into thin air."

"Ryder, who or what the hell was that?" asked Thunder.

"That was a god, and She brought us a warning, let's ride." Within moments thirty motorcycles roared from the huge garage, just as the first shell exploded on it. Hellfire rained down on the gang's headquarters, but the Chosen had escaped that fate.

A moment later they heard the helicopters closing in. The gun fire from the choppers stopped suddenly as the scream of rage and challenge from above alerted them to danger. The dragon dropped from the sky, leveling off and spitting flame. The two helicopters were engulfed and destroyed. The Chosen fled on as armored ground vehicles pursued them at speed.

The dragon stooped again, and a part of the road was blasted away, stopping some of the pursuers and slowing down the rest. The riders fled on. More military vehicles soon came in behind them from a side road.

A darkened tunnel loomed ahead. As they neared Shadow stepped out of the mouth, and with a wave of her hand created a shining disc of light over the opening. She waved them on and Ryder sped up, blasting through the portal, followed closely be her gang. Lady Shadow stepped through behind them and the portal vanished leaving the military to enter the curving tunnel far too fast.

Thirty motorcycles roared onto the dry dusty plain together. The leader spun her bike around, sending up a cloud of dirt and dust along with her wild scream of joy. "Yaaahhhhhhahahaha. Fuck, what a rush, can we do that again?"

"Perhaps later," smiled Shadow as she appeared beside Ryder. "Come with me now. Kara, Penny, see to the Chosen." With that she and Ryder vanished.

They reappeared beside the bombed-out headquarters of the bikers. "Holy crap. Lady Shadow, do you know why they came at us?"

"I have some suspicions, my sister."

Ryder was quiet for a moment the spoke softly. "Do you know why I can't contact Moragah?"

Shadow put her arm around the smaller woman's shoulders and hugged her gently. "No, I don't, nor can I reach Her myself. This is greatly disturbing to me, but we have another task at the moment. I am well aware we did not retrieve all your people. You must locate them for me now."

"Shadow, we can't go for them all, they're too spread out. It'll take too long. I'll warn them to go into hiding. That will buy us some time, time to make a plan."

"Are you certain they'll be safe?"

"Yeah, I am. Shadow, I don't think they were after the Chosen, I think they were after me."

"They were after both, Ryder, but yes, you would be their primary target. All right, warn your people, then we'll go back to Sanctuary, rest, then decide what happens next."

Ryder nodded, then pulled her phone from her pocket and called. "Ryder?"

"Run. Spread the word, I'll contact you all later."

"Running." The line went dead.

"You were prepared for something like this?"

"Lady Shadow, you know the life we lead, the things we do. There's always the possibility of an attack, cops, other gangs, somebody is always thinking about taking our scalps. The trick is to stay one step ahead."

For the first time Ryder saw the Elf warrior smile, exposing her gleaming fangs. "Ellen is going to love you. Are we ready?"

"Yup."

"Then let's go home." She created a small portal and they passed through.

AS THUNDER DISMOUNTED from his motorcycle he heard a squeal of delight. Without warning a bundle of energy leaped into his arms. He laughed and swung her around and around, finally setting her back on her feet. "Good to see you too, Angel."

Still grinning Kara turned and leaped at another rider. "Kyle," she shouted as she grabbed him in a bear hug and lifted him off his feet, bringing a grunt as the air left his lungs.

"Put me down, Jesus woman, you're killing me."

"You're getting soft, Kyle," she grinned impishly as she let him go.

"Says you. Got any beer?"

"No beer," said a cold voice nearby. Kyle turned to see a dark girl with eyes as cold as ice moving toward them. "You're the one who got her hooked on that horse piss."

Kara giggled then spoke. "Kyle, meet the missus, Lady Justice. Kyle?"

"Quiet, Angel, I'm trying to make a decision."

"A decision? What decision?"

"I don't know if I should hide behind you or run for my life."

Tasha couldn't hold it and broke out into a wide grin, her eyes dancing with merriment. "Come here and hug me, you fool." Matching her grin, Kyle opened his arms and she stepped into them. "Kara told me all about it, Kyle. You were especially good to her at a time in her life when she needed it. You'll always be my buddy for that."

"Does that mean you're not going to kick my ass for past misdeeds?"

Laughing she hugged him again then released him and stepped back, a twinkle in her eye. "We'll let it pass for now."

At that point Penny arrived with Dex in tow. She was introducing him just as Shadow and Ryder returned. "Is this all, Great Lady?" asked Dex as he knelt before her.

When she replied her voice, although soft, carried to everyone, both in the barracks and outside. "It is, for now, Dex.

"People, you are safe here, those who seek your death cannot reach you now. We are a diverse people, but we have one important thing in common. We have dedicated ourselves to the service of Moragah, Goddess of Wisdom, Defender of the Weak.

"Take this time of peace to rest, get to know one another. When I return we will gather together and decide what to do next."

"Return? Where are you going?" asked Ellen.

"To find Moragah," was the soft reply. With that, she vanished again.

Stunned, they stood staring at the place she had been standing, then they began to shake it off. Penny stepped forward. "Ellen, orders?"

Ellen laughed as Penny handed over the mantle of command. "Come on, Ryder, bring the Chosen, Dex will find accommodations for you all. Once everyone has settled in, I think we should hold a council of war."

"War?" asked Thunder.

"They brought war to us, my friend," replied Ellen. "I can assure you, Lady Shadow will accept that challenge. The leaders of these diverse groups need to meet, get to know each other, find as much common ground as possible. We have no idea how long we'll be here. This man is Dex, and he's vital to our survival here. Play nice."

WHILE ELLEN TRIED TO bring the humans together, Lady Shadow searched all the regular places where the priestesses were to be found. There was devastation everywhere. Her eyes grew hard as she saw the level of destruction and death. Those attacks had shown no consideration for human life. She'd gotten her people out, the humans they tried to protect and had to leave behind, had paid the price.

The grounds the mansion once stood on were destroyed, only a crater remained. Even the gateway to the mansion had been altered by the explosion, it was useless now. With a heavy heart, Shadow turned away and vanished.

She reappeared in a deep cavern. "Moragah, I know you can hear me. I'm safe here for the moment. Please talk to me."

Instantly she was engulfed by the vast presence of her goddess. "We have only moments, my beloved child. Are the others safe?"

"The sisters and their special people are safe on another world, Ryder and the Chosen as well. Moragah, what happened?"

"Sadly, I betrayed you, Seline."

"What? You did what? How ...?"

"Be at peace, Shadow. It was not intentional. No, the darkness is ever busy, and ever sly. It took note of the places I seemed to spend more time, expended more energy. Over time it was able to pinpoint a rough location for each priestess. From there its agents investigated until they narrowed down the target area.

"The darkness is also aware of Miranda and fears her. It managed to keep her off balance until it was ready to strike. It also fears you, you most of all. Only by staying away from you all can I protect you at this time. Be assured, I am seeking ways to counteract this. Seline, I see in your mind what you're thinking. The risk is too great."

"You told me to embrace what I am."

A wave of warm loving energy swept over her then. "Very well then, my child, be careful, and watch over them until I can return to you. You must be their purpose and comfort for now." With that She was gone. A heartbeat later, Shadow vanished.

THUNDER WAS FACING off against Dex. "I don't like it, not one damn bit."

"What you or I like, or do not like, is irrelevant, large human. The goddess gave me direction to billet the machine riders away from the others."

"Not happening. I ..."

"What's the problem here?"

"Who're you?"

Faced with an angry biker twice her size, Ellen swallowed hard, but didn't back down. "I'm Ellen, Lady Shadow's wife, companion, other half, whatever title will work for you. Who're you?"

"Name's Thunder."

"I'm not even going to ask."

"Thanks for that."

Ellen grinned, and he relaxed his shoulders a bit. "So, Thunder, what's the problem?"

"Our fussy friend here wants to put the Chosen in another barracks. It's not right. If we're here then we must have a role to play in whatever the hell is going on, otherwise Shadow would just have grabbed Ryder and left us behind. If we're not going to be accepted as equals here, then tell me now. We'll ride out as far as we can before the gas runs out then we'll work from there."

At that point Kara and Ryder arrived. "All right, what's got you worked up now, big brother?" asked Ryder. He told her. "Man's got a point, Angel."

"I agree that he does," said Ellen. "Will you let me deal with it or do you want to wait for Seline to return."

"You're the boss," grinned Kara. "Dex, this woman is precious to Lady Shadow. Your goddess often seeks this woman's wisdom. I promise you she will accept whatever decision Ellen makes here."

"But the great Lady said to ..."

"Did she say why?" asked Ellen, a twinkle in her eye.

"She said these people are somewhat less disciplined than the others. She was concerned about possible conflict."

"There'll be no conflict," said Ryder. "The Chosen defend the weak, and themselves. Yes, we can be a bit rowdy at times, but we'll keep a lid on it, I promise. Will this be acceptable to you?"

"Accepted," said Ellen. "Dex, take the Chosen to Intel. Ask him to assign them space."

"But the lady said ..."

"Dex, these folks are our allies. I'll take full responsibility for this."

"Very well. I believe you misunderstand me, Ellen. I do not fear Lady Shadow's displeasure, it's her approval I seek. I will reassign the Chosen. Come with me, large human. I'll take you to Intel. He's the leader of the soldiers."

A short time later Dex introduced them then left them to figure it out. "Odd bugger, that one," mused Thunder as they watched Dex walk away.

"Yeah, he is, but he has good reason," replied Intel.

"Oh?"

"Yeah. As I understand it, his people utterly destroyed themselves, wiped themselves out. He's the guy who invented the bomb that did it."

"Seriously? Shit man, that's a heavy load to carry. I'll let the riders know to cut him a bit of slack."

Intel nodded his approval. "Okay, so you guys want to be billeted with the rest of us. Makes sense, we're allies after all. Okay, I've got the civilians close to the doors, then the soldiers, my guys here, and Decoy's men there. The rest is open for chances. Pick your spot."

"How about down at that end, that way the bikes won't get in the way."

"You're bringing in your bikes?"

"You bring your guns and shit?"

"Bikes are part of your kit?"

"Standard issue," grinned Thunder.

"Fair enough. All engine maintenance between oh nine hundred and eighteen hundred?" he grinned at Thunder's raised eyebrow. "Nine a.m. and six p.m."

"Got it," chuckled Thunder. "I'll bring the gang." With that he walked away. Outside Shadow had returned and the sisters hurried to greet her.

A Few Moments of Peace

Shadow reappeared at the landing site and morphed back into Seline Elmore. All her sister priestesses were running toward her. "Seline, did you find Her? Is She all right?" Penny was distraught as she reached Seline, the others close behind.

Seline stepped into Penny's arms and hugged her gently. "Easy girls, easy. I'm beat to a rag. Yes, I found Moragah, She's fine. I'll tell you everything, but you have to get me in out of the heat before I perish."

With the sisters in Moragah gathered around her, Seline was escorted toward the barracks. Dex met them at the door and dropped to one knee before her. "Dex, honey, which one is my bunk? I'm beat."

"I have placed the Sisters of Shadow in the officer's quarters, along with their consorts. Did I do wrong?"

"You did fine, my friend. Lead the way."

He led them into the barracks, then through another archway. They were in somewhat more elaborate quarters. "Is this adequate, Great Lady?"

"Dex, this is perfect. Now, I need to rest. You do what you can to get everybody settled in."

"I shall do my best, my goddess. Unfortunately, the Chosen were unwilling to comply with your wishes, and insisted on being housed with the others. Ellen overruled me and so they are here. What do you wish me to do?"

"It's okay, Dex. I just thought they might prefer space to themselves, but if they want to join the rest of us I have no problems with it. Dex, I dropped a near impossible task on you and you've exceeded my expectations. Go get some rest now."

"Thank you, Great Lady. Should you have need, just call and I'll come running."

She smiled and patted his shoulder. "I know, and thank you. Get some rest now."

As he walked away she turned to take in her surroundings. They were in a large common room with doorways leading off it. The furniture was a bit large for them as Dex's species was a bit taller of stature. With a deep sigh, Seline fairly melted into an oversized chair. Ellen eased in beside her and cuddled her close. "I should put you to bed, sweet girl."

"Soon, lover," replied Seline. "Okay, girls, gather round and I'll tell you what I saw, and what I know, what Moragah said.

"First, the area of Georgia City controlled by the soldiers has been flattened, likewise the waterfront area of North Bay. Lenni's house is gone, as is the clubhouse of the Chosen. People, they came at us with everything except nukes.

"Now, for Moragah. I found Her, but we only had a few minutes together before She fled. Ladies, our goddess believes She inadvertently betrayed us."

"What???"

"Easy now. Here's where we all screwed up. Moragah is a goddess of Balance, a neutral deity. Does it not stand to reason that there is also another of the light and one of the dark? Moragah believes She has been secretly under surveillance since Penny awakened Her. The dark saw where She focused the most of Her energies. Until something changes, She will avoid us to protect us. She's working on a way to counter whatever the dark has going on, so She can come back to us.

"After we defeated the fishmen, we were expecting some sort of backlash. It took so long we relaxed our guard. They nearly caught us with our pants down. If it hadn't been for Miranda's unease I wouldn't have clued in, and things could have been a lot worse.

"Moragah told me the dark fears Miranda. Since she was instrumental in our timely escape this morning, I fully expect Lady Watcher to be a prime target for the servants of the dark."

"Yeah, and you too, Lady Shadow," sighed Miranda. "I sensed something going south in a hurry, but it was you who got everyone out in time. The dark will be after your scalp too."

"No doubt, but, we got out with our people somewhat whole."

"So, now it's time to plan out next move?" asked Lacy.

"No, Warrior, now it's time to rest and see to the comforts of our people. Go out there, make sure everyone's okay, reassure them all is well, that they're safe now. I'll sleep for a week or so, then we'll put our heads together and plan our next move."

"She's right, ladies," said Ellen. "Seline needs to rest. You all go see to your people and I'll tuck her in then join you."

Ellen led Seline to the oversized bed and sat beside her as Seline stretched out. "What is it, lover?" asked Ellen as she lightly brushed back the hair from Seleine's eyes.

"How come you always know?"

"Quit stalling and tell me what's bothering you."

Seline sighed and gazed at the ceiling. "This morning, when She brought the warning, Moragah almost seemed impatient with me."

Ellen visibly paled. "What happened?"

"She told me to stop holding back and fully embrace what I am. Ellen, I tried, am trying, but I don't really know what I am. What I do know scares the bejebbers out of me."

Ellen's voice was choked, barely audible. "Sweetie?"

"You know, Ellen, you already figured it out."

"Say it out loud, honey. Say it then we'll deal with it, you and I together like always."

Seline sighed again. "There's a god of light, one of the dark, and Moragah, a neutral. They're confined to Earth, otherwise Moragah would be here with us and the dark would have followed, but they're not here. I am. Why is that? Whatever I can imagine I can create, make real. The thing is, Ellen, the more I do, the more I can imagine.

"I'm not a god, but I'm a lot closer than I want to believe, especially now that I know they're confined to Earth, but I'm free to roam. I can go anywhere I can imagine, do anything I can imagine, and I'm starting to see the really scary part. My imagination is limitless.

"Ellen, these people, our people, can't ever know this, not ever."

"Honey?"

"I won't be the magic geni in the bottle, granting every wish. I need to help them, protect them, but make sure they do it for themselves, remain self-sufficient." Ellen nodded, not making eye contact.

"Ellen, don't you dare. Don't you even dare to think I don't need you. You have to keep me grounded, tease me, boss me around, nurture me, hen-peck me, keep me focused, and love me so hard it makes me crazy. Ellen, without you I'll never be able to survive, and without me, those people we both love and cherish won't survive either. Please ..."

Ellen leaned down and kissed her softly. "All right, sweetheart, I got it. You and me together, like always. I promise."

"Ellen, Ryder knows. When she first saw me she acknowledged me, knelt and pledged herself to me. She said she knows what I am, and I believe her."

"You get some rest, I'll go talk to her." With another soft kiss for Seline, Ellen rose and left the room.

ELLEN FOUND RYDER WITH Kara and the Chosen. "Hi folks, everything okay here?"

"All good here, Ellen," said Kara after she'd introduced everybody. "Seline catching a nap?"

"Yes. Using the juice like that takes the starch out of her. She'll sleep for a day or two then be ready to go all over again. Ryder, can I talk to you for a minute?"

"Uh, sure. What's up?"

Ellen smiled and linked her arm through Ryder's. "Come on, I want to show you something really cool. This is just for fun; all the other girls have seen it."

"Okay, sure, why not?" She allowed Ellen to lead her aside.

Ellen looked around then decided they were far enough away. "All right, I need to talk to you, and this bit of silliness is my excuse to get you alone for a minute. Okay?"

"Ellen, what's going on?"

"Watch. The other girls all have magic armor, but all I have is a disguise." With that Ellen morphed into the platinum blonde with the tan.

Ryder did a double take then clapped her hands and laughed with delight. "Wow, that rocks. Okay, so what's up?"

"Ryder, you told Lady Shadow that you know what she is, what she is capable of. Just what do you think she is? What do you think she can do?"

"She's a god, Ellen. You know that. She can do anything she can imagine, anything she wants to. Why?"

"Shadow was right, you're an extremely insightful young woman. Ryder, Shadow would like to keep that a secret for now. Have you spoken to anyone about this?"

"When she first showed up, then vanished, Thunder asked what she was. I said she was a god. I know he didn't believe me, so I said nothing more about it. So, why keep it a secret?"

"She doesn't want to be the magic geni, just granting wishes while everybody sits back taking it easy. She will help us, but ..."

"Okay, I get it. Yeah, it makes sense at that. All right, lips are sealed. It was a lot like that when the Angel first brought me to the Chosen."

"Who or what is the Angel?"

"The Fallen Angel."

"I thought that was you."

"It is, now, but back then I was a child slave. The angel brought me out, took me to the Chosen who adopted me. Later, Moragah enhanced me and I became the angel.

"I get where Shadow is coming from. I could easily do it all for the Chosen, but if I did they wouldn't be who they are. They need to do things for themselves, we all do. I'll keep my trap shut, Ellen, I promise."

"Ryder, I'm so sorry, I had no idea you were like Kara."

"Yeah, that's why I'm so hard on pedophiles, pimps, and slavers."

"I guess I'm surprised Kara didn't … she was the original Fallen Angel, wasn't she? I'm not supposed to know that, am I?"

Ryder grinned. "They told me you were the brains of the outfit. Easy to see why. So, are you going to stay blonde all day to surprise Shadow?"

"Nice change of subject, girl," smiled Ellen. "Okay, mom lecture over, you can go play now. Friends?"

"I'm honored, Ellen. Thank you."

HOURS LATER SHADOW reappeared and spoke to Dex. He hurried about, gathering all the people in the eating area. When all were seated, Lady Shadow arose. "People, we have survived. We who have dedicated our lives to defending the weak were attacked with ill intent, but we survived.

"I brought you here for safety, and for rest. I encourage you to take that rest, rest and put some thought into what you want to do next. Discuss it among yourselves, decide what you would like to do, then we, the sisters in Moragah, will sit down together with your leaders to hammer out a plan of action."

It was Thunder of the Chosen who stood and voiced what was on many minds. "Pardon my saying, but it might help if we knew what some of the options are."

"There are three main options," replied Lady Shadow. "We can return to Earth, remain here, or seek another world where we could more easily survive, prosper. That's enough to start." With that she morphed back into Seline and sat down. Dex brought her a platter of food.

"Food's over here, folks," called Becky Jordan, a soldier who had once been a waitress and Lady Warrior's getaway driver. "It's cafeteria style, so come and get it. We're not sure what tastes like what, but Dex says it's all edible."

"Hey, this one tastes like chicken," grinned Kyle as he took another bite of the strange looking vegetable on his platter. That brought a round of nervous laughter from the others.

As the meal was slowly consumed, the hum of conversation grew. Many of the people knew each other, knew of some of the others and made themselves known. Mostly, the Chosen were left to themselves at first, but Heather Jones took her plate, patted Lady Seeker on the shoulder, then approached them.

Heather sat between Marla and Kyle. "Try this one," she said, pointing to something on Marla's plate. "It really does taste like chicken."

Marla tasted the object, gave an approving nod, then swallowed. "Name's Marla. Why aren't you scared to death of me?"

"Heather. Should I be?"

"You're one of the in-crowd, the pretty people, scared to death of the likes of me, don't talk to people like me, don't even admit we're human. Aren't you afraid I'll punch your lights out, steal your stuff, or you'll catch something?"

"Nope. Try that one, I'll be darned if it doesn't actually taste like a hot dog."

Dutifully, Marla took a taste. "Well I'll be damned, so it does. Back to the why you're not afraid thing."

"You're one of the Chosen, silly woman. You people defend the weak. That's me. So, why should I be afraid one of my defenders would beat me up?"

Marla fairly roared with laughter. Heather smiled then went on. "Marla, this is a different world, literally. We've all got to work together if any of us is going to survive. I've been married to a priestess of Moragah long enough to know that the strong and the weak both have a role to play, that we need each other, now more than ever.

"Lady Shadow wants to know what we all want to do so she can make a plan. We need to find a way to support her, and the best way is to work together. I need to know what you folks want, need, so I can figure out how that can work with what we want, how to make it work for everybody."

"So, I take it you're a woman with a bit of influence here," said Kyle. "Now, here's what I need. I need Tasha to forget about my past, and I could use a few dozen beer, oh, and gas for the bike. Now, tell us what you need."

"A shopping mall and a few thousand bucks, I'll bet," said Marla.

Heather didn't rise to the bait. "Actually, I was thinking about a suit of that magic armor and a few weapons. I've been terrorized, my friends and lover threatened, hunted, my life stripped away, first by a drunk driver and now these assholes, I want some payback."

Marla suddenly grinned. "Heather, I misjudged you. You're a sister after all." All up and down the long tables it was the same as others had followed Heather's example. Several soldiers had joined them, as had the Georgia City chief of police and his wife. Heather smiled with delight as she listened to Alicia Murdock try to wheedle an interview out of Thunder.

"WELL GENERAL?"

General George Slevin eased himself in the plush leather chair facing the desk. The hard-eyed man behind that desk wasn't a public figure, yet he controlled most of the country, especially the current government, and he owned the general, body and soul. "Nothing, sir. Not a single sign of any of them anywhere, their co-conspirators either."

"What about those police officers in Georgia city?"

"Vanished, sir. Not a single sign of them."

"The reporter?"

"Nope, nothing."

"Your conclusions?"

"They may be among the dead, but I wouldn't count on it. That Lady Blue has been reported dead a hundred times over the years, yet she keeps popping up. I sometimes wonder if it's the same person, or different people using the identity. Sometimes she's a tall blonde, others a brunette, sometimes a small blonde. Who the hell knows?"

"Any sign of Lady Justice?"

"None, sir. I'm actually pretty confident we got that one."

"Explain."

"We utterly destroyed their hideout, nothing left for two city blocks, and she hasn't been seen since. I ordered my men to be somewhat brutal when questioning the locals, hoping to draw her out if she survived. Not a sign of her anywhere."

"So you're satisfied we were completely successful?"

The general sighed and looked at his hands. "No sir, not really."

"Explain."

"The report states that, after the initial strikes, Lady Shadow appeared and took some of the people out."

"Do you know who and where?"

"She got the bounty hunter and the bikers our west for sure. We've been unable to find where she took them. She was also involved in the battle on North Bay, but obviously survived that. We don't know where they are, nor can we find a single trace of them."

The hard-eyed man rose and began pacing around the huge office, his security guards on full alert. "This is distressing news. I didn't expect to get them all, but I had hoped to get Shadow and that visionary of hers. Any news of that one?"

"None, sir."

"Dammit, Slevin, this just isn't good enough. Keep up the pressure but keep as much of a lid on it as you can. This is a fucking nightmare, thank god we control the media. We can keep the political fallout to a minimum. Get out of here and find those people."

He waved his hand and the general slunk from the office with a soft, "Yes, Mr. Kaufman."

The man continued to pace. "They took my brother," he muttered. "They will pay for that. Oh yes, they will indeed pay for that."

Plots and Plans

The next morning there was a private meeting in Lady Shadow's quarters. Just the priestesses of Moragah plus Ellen, Debbie, and Viper. "All right, my sisters," said Lady Shadow, "let's put our heads together. Ellen, what happened and where do we stand?"

"Oh, well, we were taken by surprise. We were hit by full military forces, forces that we didn't see coming. Fortunately, both you and Miranda caught it just as it was happening and managed to get us out with our hides intact.

"Where we stand. We're safe on an alien planet, we have food, clothing, and shelter, so for the moment, we're good."

Shadow turned to Miranda. "Lady Watcher, have you any idea why you were unable to see that attack building up?"

"I believe I do. The soldiers weren't aware they were going into battle. They were just happy they'd been called back from overseas. They thought they were on some sort of exercise, that's why everything was so fuzzy. Once they got their marching orders it started to go black in a hurry and I could see, but it was nearly too late.

"This is all my fault, I didn't see it coming and nearly got us all killed. I really need to refine the way I search."

"There's no fault here, my sister," said Shadow as she gave Miranda a gentle hug. "Without you we'd all have been destroyed in the initial attacks. Miranda, one thing I did learn from Moragah is that the dark fears you. You were the prime target of the North Bay attack.

"So, I now find myself at a loss as to the next step. The subject is now open for discussion."

"Without Moragah to guide us, you're the boss now, Lady Shadow," said Ryder. "Tell us what you want done and we'll start figuring out how to do it."

"No, little sister, we will decide this together. Anybody?"

"I say we go back and kick some ass, find out who's behind this and make them dead," said Lady Warrior.

"Second that," said Tasha. "I want to see some justice here, if not for us then for the people who were killed in the attacks, the innocents who had nothing to do with any of this."

"Why not," agreed Lady Seeker. "I'm game for it."

"I'm in," said Viper.

Kara nodded at Penny who turned to Lady Shadow. "The Ladies Blue vote to return, bring a little justice to the home world."

"Miranda?"

"I'm in. I have a much better idea of what to look for now. They won't be able to pull this shit on me again."

"Then we're all agreed that we wish to return to Earth?"

They all nodded, then Kara spoke up. "People, before we do this, we need to be clear on our motives, our objectives. I spent a year on the dark path of vengeance, calling myself the Fallen Angel. I can tell you, you're a lot stronger when you embrace the darkness, but you lose your soul. In honesty, if this is a revenge mission then I'll sit it out."

"No, Little Sister," smiled Shadow, "we will not return for vengeance, we'll return to continue our mission, to defend the weak, to bring justice where we can. When we return I will seek the one who commanded this atrocity, the rest of you will focus on defending ..."

"We'll focus on helping you first of all," said Penny as she rose to her feet, "right, girls? What better and faster way to defend the weak is there than to remove the oppressor? Lady Shadow, you're the greatest of us. We're a unique group of people with some truly unique skills, and one mission. Until now we've mostly worked alone, but we can't do that any longer, you know this."

"Perhaps, had we not already begun to organize, this past few days might have been different, perhaps we might not have been attacked at all," said Shadow.

"Oh, that is so much bull and you know it," sighed Ryder. "Lady Shadow, without your organization, Lady Watcher and all, we'd have been nothing but a smear on the road right now. Alone we're easy prey, together, with you to lead us, we're strong, we can survive and thrive."

"Ryder's right," agreed Lady Justice. "Come on, Seline, you're the big sister here, lead us home, you know you want to."

Lady Seeker spoke next. "Girls, let's stop dancing around the hard reality here. If we keep up this pretense we won't last a week. Trust me on this. Ryder, you know what I'm saying here."

"Yeah, I do."

"Me too," said Penny.

"Okay, so you say it, Blue," grinned Ryder. "Seeker and I have been sworn to silence."

Penny chuckled. "All right, looks like I'm up. Ladies, we the priestesses of Moragah have a god among us. Lady Shadow doesn't want to ..."

"Penny, I'm not a god ..."

"The hell you're not, Lady Shadow. You might not want to accept it, but that's what you are, and you've barely begun to see the reach of your power. We, the sister here are servants of our creator goddess, but She's not here, and from what you tell us, She plans to avoid us for the time being. So be it.

"Ladies, from this point until we regain Moragah we are no longer priestesses, we're the Sisters of Shadow. Seline, we're not asking you to do everything for us, we're all more than capable of fighting our own battles, and we want to. However, we want you to lead us, now stop fooling around and take command."

Lady Shadow sighed and nodded sadly. "Is this truly what you want? If this is so then I'll do it for you, my sisters, but I will mourn bitterly the loss of our friendship."

"So, who says you're going to lose that?" asked Lady Seeker. "Listen, sister, we've always known what you are, and we all love you anyway. You can be our goddess leader as Lady Shadow, and our silly sister when you're Seline, same as always."

"Can you truly do this, my sisters?"

"We can," smiled Miranda, "and we will. Lady, we've always known and loved you for who and what you are. This will just allow us the freedom to show our devotion to you without the pretense."

"Very well then, so be it, you are now my shadow warriors. Please, I beg you, no kneeling, no praying, to me."

"Are we not allowed to honor you, sweet sister?" asked Penny.

Before Lady Shadow could respond, Kara leaped to her feet with a raised fist slapped against her left shoulder. "For Shadow, for Justice." The others leaped to their feet and copied the salute and the prayer. "For Shadow, for Justice."

"Thank you, my sisters. So, we are decided to return to Earth to bring safety and justice back to our world as best we can. Let us now go discover what our human charges desire."

DEBBIE HAD SCOOTED out ahead of the rest. A quick word to Dex and he sped away. By the time they all arrived in the cafeteria area, the rest of the people had already assembled. The Sisters of Shadow led the way, then lined up on either side of one table, leaving the center two seats for Ellen and Seline. Once they were seated, the sisters sat and so did the rest of the people. Dex nodded his approval of the new deference being shown to his goddess.

When Shadow spoke, her voice was soft, and yet it carried easily to the whole room. "Greetings, my people. The sisters and I have conferred, and we have a plan for ourselves, but now it's time to make plans for you. Please speak freely to me, I must know your thoughts and what is in your hearts. Intel?"

"Lady Shadow, we, the soldiers of Justice, are committed to the service of Lady Justice. We are her's to command, and we'll go wherever she needs us." With that he sat back down.

"Decoy?"

"Lady Shadow, I and my soldiers are yours to command as it was in North Bay." He resumed his seat.

"Thunder?"

The big man had risen to his feet. "Look, I imagine you all want to go back and start kicking ass, and that's fine. The Chosen have no issue with that as such, but I get the impression something is being overlooked here."

"And that would be?"

"You've brought some non-combatant folks here, you can't just drop folks like Morty and Mary-jo into a combat zone and expect them to survive. Now, Heather's already got her war paint on and is ready to rock and roll, but ..."

Shadow chuckled at that. "What are you suggesting, Thunder?"

"Like I said, the Chosen will ride if Ryder says ride, no question, but we'd be happier if a few folk could be left here in safety when we do."

Shadow smiled, broadly, her gleaming fangs showing. "Thunder, when I decided to bring the Chosen here I asked Dex to find you accommodations apart from the rest. I feared differences of opinion and etiquette might erupt. I have badly misjudged you and I apologize for that.

"You're correct, the sisters and I are desirous of a return to Earth to take up the cause we have all dedicated our lives to, however, we will not charge in blindly. Only after we have established a place of safety will we bring the non-combatant members of our people back to the home planet.

"Now, having said that, does anyone here not want to return?"

"That would be me," said Morty.

"Morty?" asked Lenora.

"It's all gone, Seeker," he sighed. "They blew everything I've worked for all to hell. I've got nobody back there, and nothing to go back to."

"Easy, Uncle Morty," soothed Heather as she patted his arm.

"This man has a point, people," said Shadow. "The sisters and I have a mission back there, but the risks are high. Here is safety. The rest of the planet isn't desert like this outpost, you could make good lives here in complete safety. Think about this."

"Sounds boring as shit to me," grinned Kyle.

"We soldiers would have no purpose here, Lady Shadow," said Intel. "Without purpose the madness would set in again and we'd deteriorate into nothing. No, we swore to serve Lady Justice, and that's what we'll do."

"Very well then, it's decided. Now we make a plan to accomplish a safe return. Dex?"

He appeared and knelt before her. "What would you have of me, Great Lady?"

"This complex was once a full military compound, yes?"

"It was, Lady."

"I need to know what is stored here that we could use. Dex, I see the distress on your face. My friend, I will not ask you for offensive weapons. I wouldn't ask that of you. What I need is a way to protect my people."

"Thank you, Great Lady. There are plenty of armor suits available, plus full shields."

"Full shields? Explain."

"Lady, each city of any mention had full shields. The shield generators create a dome of energy over the whole city, nothing can enter or leave without a passage being created."

"How strong are these shields?"

"From what Intel has told me of the weapons available to your enemy, nothing they have could penetrate a shield."

"So the shield is an impenetrable dome of energy?"

"More than that, Great Lady. More like a asd ewr erw erwe ..." muttering, Dex slapped at the offending translator on his tunic causing it to sputter and crackle. "Now can I ... Yes. All right, the shield is not actually a dome over the city, it's a bubble enclosing it. Therefore, the city is safe from attack from below as well."

"So, with such a generator we could enclose a city, nothing comes in and nothing goes out without we allow it?"

"Yes."

"How large is such a generator? How difficult would it be to transport, what sort of power source would it need?"

"Great lady, the late model generators are quite compact. Any two of these soldiers could carry one. They gather needed energy from sunlight."

"Well now," mused Shadow, "isn't that interesting?" She seemed lost in thought for a moment, then leaned over to speak to Ellen who nodded her assent. "Dex, can you show our people how to use the shields, to operate them plus open and close the access points?"

"Yes, of course, Great Lady. I would be honored to do so. Will you be needing armor for your troops as well?"

"Indeed so. Take Intel and all his people with you, equip them, plus train them to use the shields."

"As you command, Great Lady. Shall I put armor on the Chosen as well?"

"Yes, do so. Ryder, go with them and get outfitted." She nodded and rose to follow Dex and the soldiers.

Shadow thought for a minute more then spoke again. "Justice, I believe your city should be our first point of return. You have the people to take control of the police force, and you have people skilled with the media. These things will be needful to ally the fears of the general population once we reappear.

"Tasha, we need to know what's going on there, what we'll be facing once we return. You know the city better than anyone. Take Kara with you and go scout out the situation for me. Here, take this, keep it safe." She passed a small object to Tasha.

"What is it?"

"It creates a portal to this place. If you need to escape, or when you're ready to return, press that button there. Press it now." She did, nothing happened. "It is now keyed to you, and you alone can operate it. Kara, here's one for you. Press the button now to set it."

Kara set it then dropped it in her pocket. "That thing's not going to go off in my pocket, is it?"

"If it does," grinned Kyle, "your ass will come back without the rest of you."

Kara shook a finger at him as everybody laughed. "That's it for you, Kyle. Just for that I won't bring you back any beer."

Gearing Up

Dex led them along a broad street then turned toward another building with tall wide doors. He placed the remote against an unseen barrier, the air shimmered for a moment then he stepped forward and opened the huge doors. They slid silently aside as he triggered the remote.

Inside there was a long wide corridor with doors leading off to the left and right. Dex opened one door and led them inside. The room was huge with several layers going up. He triggered his remote and a conveyer belt appeared with row upon row of armor suits attached. He pulled one suit down and held it up for them all to see.

"This is a suit of personal armor. The Goddess Shadow and her sisters wear officer's armor such as this. This armor becomes attuned to the wearer and will expand or retreat as desired once the connection is made. Regular troops wear armor like this one."

Dex pulled down a different suit. "The difference is this armor must be triggered by a remote device like this." He held up a device that had been attached to the armor and pressed the button. He was instantly encased in the protective suit as it slid down his arm and enveloped him. He pressed the button again and the armor retreated to his hand.

He hung the suit of armor back on the rack and turned to Intel. "You and your officers will be given officer's armor. Once you have made a full connection the remote will dissolve. The regular soldiers will have to retain their remote. Lady Ryder, you and your lieutenant will also get officer's armor.

"Also, there is no need to worry about the armor fit, it will meld itself to your body and no longer be useful to another. So, let us begin."

In the end, Intel, Decoy, and Lady Justice's inner circle were in officer's armor as were Ryder and Thunder. Becky Jordan soon had the rest of the soldiers and the Chosen outfitted. They were then marched outside where Intel led them in the drill of donning and removing the armor.

Once Dex was satisfied they could use the personal safety armor he led them to another building. This one held the big shields. He carefully instructed them in the set up and use of the shields. "One shield will protect a city for generations," he said. "Take a second with you. I have never known a shield to fail, but I know not what your planet might hold, so take another for safety."

Intel thanked him then ordered several men to carry the two shields back to the barracks. As they set about the task, Ryder noticed Dex gazing at her thoughtfully. "What?"

"Your gang, the Chosen, they remind me of an elite group of police enforcers of my own people. Come with me, bring your riders."

He turned and walked away, Ryder and the Chosen right behind him. It was a long walk and they were starting to grumble when he stopped before an imposing building. Using his magic remote, Dex opened the door and led them inside. It was a garage, and it was lined with something that looked like alien motorcycles.

"Well?" he asked.

"Well what?" asked Ryder.

"dwe wegr loergsj ..." he slapped at the offending translator, "damn thing, ah, better. Of course, you don't recognize what you're looking at. These machines are my people's equivalent of your own motorcycles. They are personal transportation vehicles, called speeders, they are pursuit vehicles. Observe closely."

He reached to the first machine and flipped a switch. It began to hum and rose several inches into the air. Dex gripped the handlebar lightly and walked outside, the machine gliding obediently alongside. Once out in the open he hopped into the seat.

The machine leaped away at terrifying speed. At the end of the street he did a full back flip then returned, riding up the side of buildings and floating easily over obstacles to come to a stop right in front of Ryder. "I have now set the machine to read your DNA. Once you grasp the handles it will no longer respond to another hand, only yours."

He stepped back as her grin of delight widened. The machine was obviously built to accommodate a larger rider than her small frame, but she didn't care. She hopped easily into the saddle and reached for the handlebars. The Chosen were all trying to get a closer look. "Okay, so how does it work?"

"This lever will adjust the machine to your smaller stature." She fiddled with it for a moment and the machine obediently lowered the seat and pulled the control panel closer, making the reach for the bars more comfortable.

"Push with your right foot for speed or relax it to slow down. Use your body movements to change direction. To slow down swiftly push down with your left foot, squeezing with your left hand will speed up the process. The machine charges from sunlight, so fuel is not an issue.

"These machines are exceptionally fast, and they will function over any terrain including water. They were designed for special police forces, not for public use, although a few of the truly wealthy did have access to them. Go slowly until you get the feel of it."

His words were lost as she exploded away, the machine weaving and wobbling wildly. Dex held his breath until she tried a back flip and fell heavily to the ground. The machine came to rest beside her, waiting for her to get up and remount. He started toward her, but Thunder caught his arm and stopped him. "Give her a minute," rumbled that deep voice.

Dex looked at him incredulously, then back to see Ryder pick herself up and beat the dust from her jeans, cussing wildly the whole time. He was astounded when she leaped back on the machine and rocketed away. It was a lot steadier this time. A few back flips, a barrel roll or two, a swift climb up the side of a few buildings, then she returned, doing a full spin as she came to a hard stop.

"Whoooooo Haaa, Thunder, you gotta try one of these things, this is awesome. Dex, I love you. This is the best ever."

"You are unharmed, Lady Ryder?"

"I'll have a few bruises, but I'm good."

"Very well then, if you're certain. Shall I provide vehicles for the other riders? Is it safe to do so?"

"Oh yeah. Sure, they may fall off a time or two until they get the hang of it, but yes, please put the Chosen on these bikes."

"As you wish, Lady Ryder. I should tell you, a recruit spent weeks of training before he was allowed to mount a machine."

"So tell me, Dex, you were a scientist, right? How did you learn to ride one?"

"Can you not guess?"

"One of the wealthy families?"

"Yes. It was my grandmother who invented the blasted things. She was quite elderly when she fell off one and broke her neck. These things are extremely dangerous, Lady Ryder, but I felt the Chosen could handle them with practice. If you return to a war zone these machines plus personal armor will greatly increase your chances of survival."

Ryder stopped and turned to face him. "Dex, I know how you came to be here, I can't begin to understand your pain, but I can tell you this, all the Chosen are broken, all of us. We don't talk about it much, but we watch out for each other, we protect each other, fight for each other, help each other survive.

"We're family, not normal family, but brother and sister survivors. We don't ask anything of each other, we don't do anything to each other, and we watch out for each other.

"Thunder, get this man some colors. He's earned them." Thunder nodded his agreement.

"Lady Ryder, what are you saying?"

"I'm saying welcome to the Chosen, Dex. You're as broken as the rest of us and I'll ride with you any day. You're welcome if you want to ride with us."

He seemed to be somewhat overcome. "I would be honored, Lady Ryder, truly, but ..."

"I too serve the goddess Shadow, as do the Chosen now. There's no conflict here. So, what'll it be, want your colors?" He just swallowed hard and nodded eagerly, not trusting his voice. "Kyle, you still got that extra jacket on your bike?"

"Sure do. We got a new rider?"

"That we do."

Kyle took off his leather jacket and held it out for Dex. Kyle was a big man and the jacket wasn't a bad fit. Dex was smiling as he flexed his broad shoulders in the leather, then he saw Kyle holding out his hand. "Welcome, Brother."

"Thank you, Brother," Dex replied softly. "Come, let's get you on a real mount."

By the time the evening meal rolled around the Chosen looked like they'd been in a brawl. There were bruises and scrapes everywhere. Intel grinned at Thunder. "Looks like you folks traded up," he said as he nodded at the new bikes.

"That we did. These things are a serious upgrade. Take a bit of getting used to though."

"Looks like you've got a new recruit too."

"Ah huh. You know how he got here, that much alone makes him Chosen. He's a hell of a rider though, makes one of those machines do all kinds of wild and interesting things." Intel nodded his approval. "So, you guys have fun playing with your new toys?"

"You know it," grinned Intel. "We'll be a lot more effective when we get back. I just wish Dex would share a few weapons."

"Naw, he won't do it, Intel. He'll give you armor, shields, he may even have some other defensive tricks up his sleeve, but he's sworn to keep as many alive as possible."

"Is that why you guys adopted him?"

"The only thing worse than being broken is carrying that load alone. He'll be safe with us, nobody'll ever ask him about it, nobody will ever hassle him. He'll be safe, inside, never alone again. That's the magic and the beauty of the Chosen."

"I get that, Thunder, I do. It's the same for the military. All my people are vets, broken, abandoned, and alone. They find their way to me and I try to bring them back, help them find themselves again. I guess the Chosen aren't so different from the rest of us after all."

"Maybe not, but we got cooler bikes," chuckled Thunder.

Intel laughed with him. "Yeah, can't argue that."

"You're fussing, what's up?"

"Lady J and Little Blue went back to scout out the city."

"It's hard, isn't it?"

"You mean not doing it all for them, but just sitting around waiting for them and trusting them to get it done?"

"Yeah, that. I get it. Come on, Ryder always says when there's nothing to do then you might as well eat and sleep. Let's see what kind of alien grub they've got for us this time."

The two men walked into the cafeteria area together.

Scouts

L ady Shadow walked outside with Kara and Tasha. They watched Dex lead the soldiers away then turned back. "Where, Tasha?"

"The sewers, Lady Shadow, well away from the hideout."

"So be it. Take no chances, my sisters, but learn as much as you can."

"We will," replied Tasha, "this could take a few days. Don't start worrying for at least a week."

Shadow grinned at that. "Kara, keep a rein on her, will you?"

"Count on it," grinned Kara as she took Tasha by the hand. "Let's go."

Lady Shadow created the portal and they stepped through. As she stood watching the place where they disappeared, Lady Blue approached. "You're concerned for you mother and grandmother in New York."

"Yes, I am. Seline, could I ..."

"Come, we'll go together." She created the portal and they stepped through.

Magda Larson had been gazing through the window, fretting that she couldn't reach Penny, when a bright light appeared in the driveway and Penny stepped through with a strange looking companion. She hurried to the door to find them standing there, Penny's arm raised to knock.

"Inside, quickly now." The old woman ushered them in, took a quick look to see if they had been observed, then closed the door and hugged Penny tightly.

"Grandmamma, oh Gran, it's so good to see you safe and sound."

"I'm fine, Penny. It was you I was worried about. Perhaps I'm getting paranoid in my old age, but I sometimes wonder if the house is being watched." She released Penny and turned to Shadow. "You're Lady Shadow," she said as she bowed her head.

"I am honored to meet you, Magda Larson. We feared the worst, but it appears to be unnecessary. Penny has kept her secrets well. New York seems to have escaped attack. Your home is not being watched."

"Attack? The news said there was a terrible outbreak of disease in North Bay. It's been cordoned off by the military. We tried and tried to reach Penny but couldn't. I do admit we were getting frantic with worry. Come, ladies. We'll have tea and catch up."

"Where's Mamma?"

"Out trying to quietly gather information, Penny, to find out what has happened to you."

"Call her home, right now. She can't give a single hint that she knows anyone in North Bay."

"Of course. You put the kettle on and I'll call Mary." Magda stepped away to place the call and Penny dutifully put the kettle on. Lady Shadow pressed a portal device into Penny's hand then vanished. Magda returned to find Penny alone, smiling at her. "Did she vanish into thin air?"

"Yes, actually, she did," grinned Penny. "Is Mamma on her way home?"

"She'll be here in a few minutes. Penny, what's going on, can you tell us?"

"Once Mama's here I'll fill you in, but then I'll have to return to Shadow. Now, it's been too long, tell me what all you've been up to."

WHILE PENNY WAS HAVING tea with her mother and grandmother, Kara and Tasha were huddled together in the sewers.

Kara was struggling to keep Tasha from going on the warpath. "No, Tash honey, not yet."

"They just killed them all, Kara. They blew up everything for blocks. Now they're terrorizing, letting the street gangs run wild. All the people, all the innocent people, I swear, there will be a reckoning for this madness. I swear there will be justice for this."

"There will, sweetheart, there will. I'll help you, so will the sisters, our soldiers. We have to do it right, though. We can't do this by ourselves, we can't."

"The Fallen Angel could."

"Maybe." Kara sighed. "Is that what you want, Tasha? You want me to embrace my dark side and cut loose all over the military?"

Tasha grabbed Kara and hugged her tightly, tears of impotent rage flowing down her face. "No, Kara, no. I won't ever ask that of you, I won't. I'm just gutted here, what they've done is tearing me apart. Please help me, I'm so lost."

"Hush now, hush, Momma Kara's got you, sweet Tasha, you're safe here with me. Honey, we won't let this pass, we won't. Tasha, I promise you, we'll make this right, and if there's no other way, I will unleash the Angel. This will not go unavenged."

"No, Kara, no, I ..."

"Hush now, hush and let me hold you. We'll wait until dark then we'll move out into the rest of the city, see what else we can see. We need to know where the enemy soldiers are, their numbers, weapons, etc. We need to know what's going on with the police, the media, and everything else we can find out."

"Kara?"

"Yes honey?"

"Please don't ever tell anybody what a sad mess I am most of the time. It'll ruin Lady J's reputation."

"Not a word," giggled Kara, "as long as I get a snuggle a day your secret is safe with me."

"You nut," smiled Tasha, the rage that threatened to consume her pulling back at last. "Fine, we'll snuggle here until darkness falls then we go hunting."

"Good plan, I like it. Tash, we can't let the enemy know we're back. We've got to keep our true identity secret until Shadow is ready."

"Yeah, you're right, we just pledged to a new goddess, best not to piss Her off on the first mission."

Kara giggled at that and cuddled Tasha closer. Silently she vowed to unleash the Fallen Angel if there was no other way. If all else failed, she would burn the enemy down. The Angel would bring hell to Earth in retribution. One way or the other Tasha would see justice done.

Night approached, and they began to stir. They climbed the ladder and pushed aside the manhole cover. Silently they slipped out onto the street. As the evening wore on they saw the streets patrolled by armed soldiers. By ten o'clock the streets were empty. Curfew. They climbed to the rooftops and scouted the city.

They saw a few shadowy figures slinking about as people tried to move around without being caught. After a while they spotted a police car. The big cop was harassing a teenager he'd cornered. "You're in deep shit now, boy. You're out after curfew. You know what happens next."

The boy swallowed hard, looking over the cop's shoulder. "Justice."

"That's right, justice. I'm taking you to the MPs."

"No. Lady Justice," said the boy. "Behind you."

The policeman spun around, reaching for his gun, but his hand stopped halfway to it as he saw Tasha standing there, her eyes cold as ice.

"Boy, get lost. I was never here." The teenager nodded then ran. "Hey, Martin, long time, no see."

He gulped and brought his hand away from the gun. "Lady Justice. We thought you were dead."

"Sorry to disappoint."

He sighed and visibly relaxed his shoulders. "I'm not disappointed, Lady Justice, I'm relieved. Things have gone all to hell in this city without you."

"Tell me."

"The military is everywhere, interrogating everyone, and they're not being gentle about it either, plus they're letting the street gangs and dealers run rampant. Girl, they're trying to flush you out. They've got heavy weapons, every interrogation, every brutal action on the street, is done with the hope you'll try to interfere. It's all bait, Lady J, bait to catch you out and kill you. Get out of town, lay low for a while until they pull out."

"Why Martin, I didn't know you cared."

"Look, you scare the shit out of me, I'll admit that, but you also saved my life. I owe you. Besides, life in this city was a lot better when you were here. At least then people could walk the streets. Now, they just grab people for no reason."

"That remind you of anything?"

He sighed deeply, not meeting her eyes. "Yeah, it does. Look, ever since you pulled me out of the sewers that time, I've been trying to live up to your standards. I admit I've behaved like an asshole, and I'm trying to make amends."

"So, make amends, help me. Tell me everything you can about the situation as it stands."

He nodded slowly. "Okay. We're under martial law. There's a curfew that they enforce. The police are under the command of the military. They've appointed a new chief, lieutenant, and sergeant, MPs all. We spend our days searching for you with orders to shoot on sight, shoot to kill."

"How many troops?" asked Kara as she suddenly appeared beside Tasha.

"You're Lady Blue. As far as I know there's three hundred soldiers deployed to run the city. Half are in the temporary camp just outside city limits, the rest are scattered around the city. Ladies, they blew the old military quarter all to hell. There's only about a dozen people who escaped that attack."

"I know," said Tasha. "I saw. There'll be a day of reckoning for that."

"What about the media?" asked Kara.

"Under military control, pumping out a steady stream of bullshit. There's a dangerous terrorist group operating out of the city, there's a deadly virus, that sort of crap. It's all just an excuse, somebody with a serious level of influence wants you dead. That's what this is all about, nothing more."

"Thanks, Martin. Oh, we never had this conversation, you didn't see anything unusual tonight."

He nodded. As she stepped back towards the shadows he called out. "Lady Justice." She stopped and turned back to face him with a raised eyebrow. "I'm glad you're okay. Welcome home." She smiled as she vanished into the shadows. He glanced around, but Lady Blue had disappeared as well.

Martin Johnson was smiling as he got back in his police car. "Car 34 reporting in."

"Base here, 34. Did you catch the perp?"

"Negative. Skinny teenager one, overweight cop, zero. I'm out of shape."

The voice on the radio chuckled. "Roger that. Go back to patrolling, 34."

"Understood. 34 out."

IT WAS IN THE POORER part of town, near where the old military zone once was. There were people huddled in the shadows, avoiding the military trucks patrolling the area. The mission doors were open, and the interior was over-crowded with dozens of street people. Near the door, a tall woman held her breath as she watched a shadow move silently along the wall, drawing closer.

As the figure came closer she recognized it and put a finger to her lips for silence. Furtively, she looked around, then opened the blanket she had wrapped around her. The figure slipped closer and moved into the blanket with her. She put her lips to the young woman's ear and whispered softly. "Thank god you're still alive. They're searching everywhere for you."

"I know," came the soft answer. "Amelda, I'm so glad you survived. Are you all right?"

"As much as can be under the current circumstances."

"Monica?"

"Her sister came and got her out. Tasha, you need to be as far away from here as you can get."

"Going now. Amelda, I'll be back soon with friends. Hang on just a little longer." With that she vanished into the shadows once again.

Not far away Kara was doing something she'd promised herself she'd never do again. She was loosening her iron grip on the Fallen Angel's rage. Tasha arrived to see Kara, in full battle armor, step in front of a jeep. As it screeched to a halt she seized it and hurled it into a building. She grabbed one of the men crawling out and slammed him against the jeep, knocking him unconscious.

The second occupant of the jeep had reached the ground, but Kara had him instantly. *"Tell me what your orders are."*

The voice wasn't human, and he was unable to resist the command. "Find Lady Justice, find Lady Blue. Kill them on sight."

"Who is in command of this operation?"

"General George Slevin."

"You hit your head when the jeep crashed. You remember nothing more. You will never speak of seeing me." She dropped him then and fled into the night. Tasha found her a few minutes later.

"Kara?"

"Right here."

Tasha settled down beside her under the huge tree. They were well hidden in the shadows. "Kara, what was that?"

"What was what?"

"That voice?"

"The voice of command," she sighed. "Nobody can resist it. It was one of the Angel's favorite weapons."

"Holy shit. I've never heard you use that before."

"I don't really like to, I feel like it comes from a dark place. I guess it doesn't really or Moragah wouldn't have given it to me, but it puts me in a dark head space."

"Then why did you do it, sweetie?"

"We need information, Tash, all we can get. Our Lady Shadow will want to know who's in command here, that will put Her on the scent of whoever is pulling the strings."

"Yeah, you're right about that."

"So, should we head back now?"

"No, there's a few more neighborhoods I want to see. We've checked on the old territory, the homeless folk etc., now I want to look at some of the better neighborhoods. What are they doing there?"

"Lead on. I'm with you all the way."

"Thank the gods for that," smiled Tasha as she led the way back to more open streets. Nothing was moving, no pedestrians, no cars or trucks, just the military and the police. They slipped around through much of the night, then broke into an empty house and settled down to rest. The next night they went out again.

By dawn they had moved up into the more affluent neighborhoods. This time they slept in an unlocked guest cabin at the back of a large estate. It was still daylight when they awakened. With the ease of a squirrel, Kara scaled a tall tree, took a quick look around then dropped back to the ground.

"See anything interesting?"

"Yeah, I did, Tash. They're still after us all right. I could see lots of military activity down on the mean streets, but almost nothing up here in the hills. If they're patrolling up here, I couldn't see them."

"Okay, so they're focusing on the mean streets, hunting for us. Now we know where they're concentrated. What's next?"

"Now we find the main encampment outside of town. From there we'll know how to cut off reinforcements to the ones down on the streets."

"Intel's going to love you. Let's go."

As darkness fell they drifted back down towards the center of town. It didn't take long to find a military truck heading in the right direction. That truck had dropped off a load of passengers to a checkpoint and was taking the relieved soldiers back to the camp. Nobody noticed that it had suddenly picked up two extra passengers.

The truck rumbled on for a way then turned off on a side street leading into a park. The military camp could be easily seen. Two shadows abandoned the truck and reunited in the trees. "You know where we are, Tash?"

"Sure do. We're in the park. Mom and Dad used to bring me here all the time when I was little. I think we're good now, we should go back and report in to Lady Shadow."

"Works for me," replied Kara, pulling the portal device from her pocket. She created the shining portal and they stepped through. It disappeared behind them.

Tasha and Kara entered the barracks just as the evening meal was finishing up. "Wow, that looks good," grinned Kara. "Did Kyle save us any, or did he eat it all?"

"Sorry, Angel, you're out of luck. You bring back any beer?"

"Tried, but they carded me and threw me out." That brought a round of laughter.

They approached the head table and Tasha gave Lady Shadow the fist to shoulder salute. "For Shadow, for freedom."

Shadow rose to her feet, smiling, and returned the salute. "For Justice, for freedom. So, my sisters, what have you learned?"

"Lots," replied Kara as she spread a city map out on the table.

"A city map?" asked Tasha, giving Kara a raised eyebrow.

"I thought it might be useful. Okay, so I stole it. Shoot me."

Tasha grinned and kissed her cheek. "Gods you're cute when you're fierce."

"Save it, girls," smiled Shadow. "Show us what you've learned. Intel, Decoy, you need to see this."

"This area here," said Kara as she circled a section of the map with her finger, "thanks." Dex had passed her a marker. She marked the area in red. "As I was saying, this area is nothing but rubble. From here to here is heavily patrolled. They have a curfew in place and they enforce it. The more upscale areas are pretty much ignored.

"The main encampment is in the park just outside the city, here. There are about three hundred troops stationed there, approximately half in the camp and half on patrol in the city at any given time. All patrols are heavily armed, and they play rough, trying to draw Tasha out for an easy kill."

"This is great intel," said Decoy. "Good job, ladies. Good job."

"There's one more thing," said Kara. "Shadow, the man in command is a General George Sleven, but we got the sense he answers to someone higher up. There's only one reason a full general would have his boots on the ground, personally overseeing an operation like this."

"His master has ordered him to do so," snarled Lady Shadow. "I shall want a word with the good general, and soon. All right, we have useful intelligence, what's our next move, Intel? How should we approach this?"

"What are the objectives, Lady Shadow?"

"I want to retake the city, bring all our people home, make that city safe. I can continue my mission from Georgia City as easily as from North Bay."

"So, we're not retaking North Bay?"

"We will, Decoy," replied Shadow, "but first, we re-take Georgia City, put Tasha and Intel back in control of the area, then we reclaim North Bay. So, Intel?"

"I'd like to slip in and set up the shield with the main camp outside the field of effect, cut their forces in half. Dex?"

Dex hurried to the people gathered around the map. "Yes?"

"Can we adjust the shield to include this main area of the city, but leave this area here on the outside?"

"Yes, of course. You will need to plant it in this area here."

"Well, that's handy," grinned Lady Justice.

"Why, Tasha, what's there?"

"There's an old bomb shelter there in a guy's backyard. I caught him dragging a girl down there and snapped his neck. The place has been empty ever since."

"Perfect," grinned Intel. "That's our incursion point."

"Prepare then, we will go at dawn."

At that point, Ryder spoke up. "Lady Shadow."

"Yes?"

"This is a military operation, no place for a wild bunch of free riders. You have non-combatants here. How about we leave some of the Chosen behind to guard them."

"Actually, I'd like to leave all the Chosen behind on this operation. I have a different task for you and your merry band of free riders."

"As you wish. What can we do to help?"

"I need you to return to the west and acquire a car. Viper sacrificed his in the battle for our escape."

"You want me to steal a car?"

"I care not at all how you acquire it. Just get it and bring it back here. I see Dex wearing Chosen colors, he can modify the car to help Vic better survive, then I want you to ride with him as he cleans out the street gangs and drug dealers from the city once we re-take it.

"The people will be safe enough here. Ellen will organize things in preparation for their return to a city under our control. Will you do this for me?"

Ryder grinned with delight. "With extreme pleasure, Lady Shadow."

"Then you will have a need for this," said Shadow as she passed Ryder a portal controller. "Dex, will you remain behind here, or will you accompany Ryder?"

Dex knelt before the warrior Elf. "With permission, Great Lady, I should like to ride with my new brothers and sisters."

Lady Shadow smiled and raised him to his feet. "So be it. Make sure they have armor, Dex, keep them safe."

"I will, Great Lady, I swear it."

Reclaiming the City

D awn was just breaking when the soldier stepped out of his tent to see the general facing the rising sun. "Morning General, you're up early."

"Couldn't sleep, Major."

"Sir?"

"We're spinning our wheels here, and I'm catching shit for it. We've taken this city, been more than nasty about it, but nothing, not a gig. You know, I'm starting to think we may have gotten lucky here. If that kid was still alive, there's no way in hell she'd have let the things we've done pass. She'd have come after us.

"No, Major, we're getting nowhere here. We'll shift our focus to North Bay. Recall your men. We'll leave our MPs in command of the police force here, let them maintain control. We'll move our operations to North Bay, see if we can get a rise out of that Shadow woman."

"Yes, Sir."

The Major spoke into his communicator for a moment. "The men are on their way, General. As soon as they arrive we'll break camp and move out. I'll ..." His radio squawked, and he responded. "Sweet Jesus Christ."

The general turned to face him. "What is it, Major?"

"Sir, there seems to be some kind of invisible barrier around the city. The men can't get out."

"What???"

"That's what they're saying, Sir."

"Get in that damned jeep, we're going to find, and court martial, those men. Christ almighty. An invisible barrier? What the hell have they been smoking anyway?"

The angry general was in the jeep with the major driving. They were barely out of the camp when the jeep slammed into an invisible wall, coming to an abrupt halt and tossing the general out over the hood to break his nose against the alien shield. The major's radio was squawking again and, angrily, he answered.

"What is it now?" sputtered the general, holding his batter nose.

"The men are under attack now sir."

"Under attack? By who?"

"They say aliens, alien soldiers led by Lady Justice."

THEY GATHERED JUST before dawn, the soldiers fully armed and wearing armor. Lady Shadow stood ready to deploy the portal. "Justice, this is your city, take command here."

"Me?"

"It's your city, Tasha. You have the sisters, and you have your troops, take back your city."

"Okay, if you say so. Intel, take Lady Shadow and your troops, get the shield in place ASAP. Decoy, take your men and set up defenses around what's left of the Military quarter, I don't want those people being used as hostages.

"Lacy, take Miranda and that hit squad of yours, re-take the TV station, install Alli there, then start pegging off any officers and small groups you can find. Penny, you and Lenora go with Decoy just in case. Kara and I'll take down the police headquarters then fetch the chief, Jess, and Sergeant Murdock, put them back in command of their own force.

"Once we've re-taken the city I'd like to see Viper make a swing through for a week or so to clean out the gangs and dealers.

"All right, let's go."

Lady Shadow created the portal and leaped through, the sisters close behind, then the soldiers, followed by the two men carrying the shield generator and Alicia Murdock. The sun was just starting to rise as they appeared beside the empty house.

Swiftly the armored soldiers swept through the building but met no resistance. The generator was set up on the neglected patio and the switch turned on. "Well?"

"It's running, and set like Dex showed us, Colonel. No idea if it's actually doing anything or not."

"Remain here," said Lady Shadow, "I'll find out. Aeroth." The dragon appeared, and she leaped to its back. They flew off, but soon returned. She was grinning.

"Lady?"

"Intel, I was gifted with the vision of a jeep slamming into the shield, throwing its occupants out over the hood. The shield is fully functional."

"Good news indeed, Lady Shadow. Blockade, we'll commandeer that house for our temporary headquarters. Take a detail and start getting us set up. Finder, get us a phone hook-up, and some internet access in there. We'll need a few other things, desks, maps, file cabinets, the usual. See if the basement is big enough to use for stores. Oh, contact Lady Warrior and see if she can steal us some reliable transportation."

"On it, Sir," grinned Finder as he saluted then trotted away. They were starting to hear gunfire deep in the city.

THE POLICE STATION had come alive with radio calls claiming that an unseen barrier surrounded the city. Even the military was helpless against it. Stuck on front desk duty, Officer Martin Johnson leaned his elbows on said desk and grinned to himself. He had a good idea what was happening.

"What the hell are you smirking about, Johnson?" demanded the Military officer in charge of the police force.

"Just happy that I'm about to see the last of you and your kind."

The MP officer stepped closer, threateningly. "And just what the hell is that supposed to mean?"

"You have no idea all what's coming, do you?"

"Suppose you tell me what you think is going on, smartass."

"I think Lady Justice has returned, I think she's pissed, and I think she's brought friends."

"Oh do you now?"

"He's not wrong," said a soft feminine voice. The MP spun around to see Tasha in full painted armor. He whipped out a gun and emptied a clip at her, but she shrugged it off. Suddenly the gun in his hand was too hot and he hissed in pain as he dropped it.

Several more guns began firing at her, but, again, she ignored it, and then a cyclone struck. A small warrior in full battle armor with blue spirals on it attacked. Bodies and weapons were hurled in all directions. Men and women lay groaning and nursing injuries as Kara came down off combat mode.

As they lay glaring at her, the warrior turned to Lady Justice. "That's all of them, the building is secure."

"Thank you, my Lady Blue. Officer Johnson, I've taken control of this facility. Gather all police officers in the meeting room, oh, and throw those three MPs in cells, would you."

"With pleasure, Lady Justice." He swiftly set about the task. Kara disappeared through a portal.

Within minutes they were gathered, and Tasha dropped her armor as she addressed them. "Police of Georgia City, you and I have been at odds for some time now. Those days have passed. The Soldiers of Justice have recaptured the city; I'm now in command here."

She gave them a minute to absorb that bit of information, then went on. "Recently, a military strike was organized against me and my people. It killed and injured many civilians, but wasn't successful in its main objective, my death and the elimination of my soldiers.

"We've returned, we've taken the city, and we will maintain control here. Any of you who hold a grudge from before, feel that you can't work with me, or have any illusions about your chances of bringing me down for the reward, take off that uniform, leave this building, and head towards the park. You'll be escorted to safety outside the city. Stay here and screw around, you will face my justice. Choose now, choose wisely."

Nobody moved for several moments then one burly policeman stood up and removed his jacket. "Fuck it, it's not worth my life." That began the rush to the doors. Casting aside hats and badges, over two dozen men fled the building. Nine officers were left seated, four women and five men.

"So, this is it then, fair enough. Officer Johnson."

"Yes, Ma'am?"

"When the attack came we took the chief, the lieutenant, and the sergeant, out with our people. It was obvious they'd lost control. I'll return control of the police force to them as soon as they arrive. In the meantime, call every off-duty police officer and anyone else you can think of, tell them what's happened here. Tell them to work with me or leave the city."

"On it," he said as he returned to the front desk and set to work.

Just then a bright light appeared, and four figures stepped out of it then it disappeared. "Chief, the building is secure, you can take over now. I'm afraid I've reduced you to a skeleton crew, but the Soldiers of Justice will work with you until you can bring your numbers back up.

"Come, Lady Blue, we have work to do elsewhere." With that both Tasha and Kara shifted onto combat mode and vanished from the building.

WHILE LADY JUSTICE reclaimed the police station and reinstated the chief, Jessica, and Bill Murdock, Lady Warrior was making herself known in the city. They stole a military jeep and sped away. Their first stop had been the TV station where they dropped off Miranda and Alicia Murdock. The Watcher swept through the building, clearing away all military personnel. Those were seen leaving the building, nursing bruises and more.

The Media was once again in control of their own fate. While the armored Watcher and her dragon made sure the building remained free of military influence, Alicia Murdock went on the air.

"Good morning, Georgia City, this is Alicia Murdock reporting from the news desk. In the early hours of this morning, the military invaders of our fair city suffered a devastating defeat. Led by Lady Justice, the Soldiers of Justice have retaken the city.

"We remain under martial law, but with a difference. The brutal interrogations will no longer be tolerated, the city has been shielded and can no longer be affected by standard military weapons, including heavy bombs. The shield prevents anyone from entering or leaving the city without permission. Please be patient and remain inside while the former captors are rounded up and expelled from within the defensive perimeter.

"In addition, please avoid trying to leave the city until proper check points are set up and manned. We fully understand we will be a city under siege, and any citizen who desires to leave will be allowed to do so once proper order has been restored. Also, we have been assured that control will be returned to the Georgia City Police Force.

"Lady Justice has assured this reporter that the city will be made safe once again, and that she has returned fully prepared to defend it properly. In her own words, "Justice will prevail on the streets and in the homes of Georgia City.""

That broadcast kept repeating until more news began to filter in. Each time there was a new development, Alicia went back on the air.

IT DIDN'T TAKE LACY long to find a troop of soldiers harassing some civilians. They were heavily armed and ready for a quick kill on Lady Justice, but they weren't prepared for a fully armored Warrior. They opened fire on her, but Lacy swept through them like wildfire. Soon all were down, and she had the keys to the military truck. Her squad quickly disarmed the downed soldiers. They were now better armed as well as fully armored.

"Here's the keys to the jeep," said Lacy. "Take it and head back to your main camp. You won't be able to reach it but get as close as you can and behave yourself. Fuck around and I'll come after you with extreme prejudice." She watched as they struggled into the vehicle and drove away. She and her crew boarded the truck and went on the hunt for more troops, they weren't hard to find.

By nightfall all the troops in the city had been rounded up and moved toward the shield, as close to their own camp as they could get. The Soldiers of Justice were now far better armed than before, and more mobile. Near the main military camp, the captured soldiers waited, separated from their fellows by the impenetrable shield.

Outside the shield there was a military buildup under way. The general was pulling all his troops from North Bay to Georgia City. He was also bringing in heavy weapons, artillery, tanks, etc. He meant to retake the city. "I'll call in nukes if I have to," he said into the phone.

"Don't be an idiot," was the harsh reply from the phone. "We dare not use that kind of weapon against our own people, at least not yet. If our enemies abroad think we're that desperate, they'll strike at us in a heartbeat. Get a grip and get this done. You know your quarry is within your reach now, and I'll bet the rest of them are with her.

"You have the opportunity to eliminate them all at once. Get it done and quietly as possible. I'll circulate a story about a deadly virus, quarantine the city. The media will spread it, leaving you free to do your job. Now get busy." The connection went dead, and, with a snarl of impotent rage, the general hurled his phone across the tent.

Inside the shield, and just out of sight, two women sat beneath a tree, one slightly distracted, the other keeping watch. Finally, as the general tossed aside his phone, Lady Seeker shook of the spell and refocused on the world at hand. "Okay, they'll come at us hard and soon, but they can't use nukes. They're going to run the old *deadly virus* story as an excuse to keep the city under wraps."

"Okay, that means we're good. From what Dex said, even the nukes wouldn't penetrate the shield, none of what they bring will do any harm. We should report back to Tasha."

"Let's go."

"Lenni, do you find it weird that Shadow put Tasha in charge?"

"Nope, makes sense to me."

"Really?"

"Think about it, Lacy. If Shadow takes over completely, we lose our confidence, and depend completely on her. This is Tasha's city. The people here know about her, what she's all about, they'll trust that. If Tasha takes back the city, she'll be confident in holding it if Shadow is called away somewhere."

"Yeah, that makes sense. See, that's why I hang out with you, you're not only super cute, but you're smart too."

Lenora laughed at that. "And I thought you just wanted another snuggle under the stars."

"Tempting as that is, I got in way too much trouble the last time I snuggled you." Lenora was still laughing as they returned to the newly christened headquarters.

"Well, you two seem to be in fine spirits, you have good news?" asked Lady Shadow. Lenora gave her a full report. "So, then we seem to be secure, but the coming days will test the shields for certain. Tell me, Lenora, how is it you were able to tune in the general? What was the connection?"

"Lacy gave me a picture of the man," replied Lady Seeker as she passed the photo to Lady Shadow.

"Warrior, where did you come by this?"

"I thought you might want to know what the man looked like, so every time we took down a troop of soldiers I asked for a picture of the general. Eventually I got lucky."

"What I don't understand, is why you asked that gal her bra size," said Omay, one of Lady Warrior's favorite snipers.

"Excuse me?" said Miranda as she faced Lacy with her fists on her hips. "Care to explain this, Lacy?"

"Dammit, Omay, you'll get me killed. Okay, I'll explain. It's an interrogation technique."

"Really? That's your story?"

"Sure. They're all pumped to be questioned for military information, ready to grit their teeth and give you name rank and serial number. I looked right at her boobs, licked my lips, and asked her bra size as I reached toward her buttons. She had the picture out in a heartbeat."

"Really?"

"Honest, works every time."

"Oh yeah? Just how many times have you tested this theory?"

"Shit. Miranda, honey, ..."

"Lacy."

"Yes?"

"34B, that's all the information you'll ever need from now on, got it?" Everybody was laughing now and Lacy was blushing crimson.

"Gods woman, you're brutal," sighed Lacy as she pulled a laughing Miranda into her arms.

"You are so much fun to tease, Lacy," said Miranda as she snuggled deeper into Lacy's arms.

"Lucky for me I wear red well, but I'm still going to beat up Omay."

"Whoa there, save it," said Omay, backing away with a wide grin. "Can't beat me up now, I'm on guard duty, right Colonel?"

"Go," grinned Intel. With a laugh of delight, Omay fled. "Okay, so what's our next move, Lady J?"

"Everybody get some rest. They'll come at us tomorrow, dealing with that is a job for soldiers. Right now, I plan to go on patrol."

"Boss?"

"I want this city to know Lady Justice has returned. I know the military let the gangs and worse run loose before curfew, but I won't. I have a good idea where they'll be throwing their weight around. I'll be back before dawn."

She saw the look on his face and softened. "Look, Intel, you have a far better idea of what needs to happen tomorrow, you're the commander of the Soldiers of Justice. Work up a plan and tell me what you need from me when I get back. Right now I have to re-establish the persona of Lady Justice. At the moment I'm nothing more than a news story, by morning I'll be the dreaded vigilante again. The people will know for certain I'm back."

He nodded his acquiescence, she was making perfect sense. As she turned to go Lady Shadow was standing in her path. Shadow reached out and took her by the shoulders. "Tasha, I'm so very proud of you. I always knew you had the makings of a fine leader."

"You do know that I'm scared to death, and making it up as I go along?"

"Yes, I do," smiled Shadow as she gave the girl a gentle hug. "So am I." She chuckled then stepped aside to let her pass.

"Come on, honey," said Kara as she took Tasha by the arm. "Let's go beat up a few bad guys." They were back by midnight. Any doubts about the return of Lady Justice had been removed.

Getting Organized

The alarm sounded at dawn, followed quickly by the sounds of explosions. A rain of shell fire exploded against the shield along with rocket fire from the air support, all to no avail. At first those who had gathered near the shield, fled from the impact points, but the Soldiers of Justice managed to gain control and restore order.

Only then did it become clear that nothing had pierced the shield. By mid afternoon most people of the city were outside watching the fireworks. By the time the sun was setting, Tasha, in her make-up and cape, was addressing the captured soldiers near the shield. Alicia and a cameraman were on hand to record everything.

The captured soldiers were getting their first real look at Lady Justice, and the tightly controlled rage she exuded wasn't reassuring them. She stopped pacing and faced them, talking through a speaker system Finder had set up for her.

"Hear me, you people are prisoners of war, my prisoners. You invaded my city and abused my people. This does not endear you to me. There needs to be some justice here for the citizens of Georgia City. So, let's consider this. You were held beside the shield, your commanders on the other side knew exactly where you were, and yet they concentrated their fire on that very spot where you stood.

"They did this because, had the shield failed, it would give them the quickest access to the city, to destroy it. Consider what your fate would have been had they succeeded in their quest, had the shield failed. Think about that.

"Now, think about this, my soldiers are all armored. This armor, as you know from experience, is impervious to any weapon your military possesses. And yet, you're all still alive, you lost not a single life to my soldiers, although Lady Warrior was all for ending the lot of you.

"Our original intention was to return you to your people, and it still is. However, your commanders aren't making that easy. I want an officer from your number to carry my demands through the shield."

"This country will never negotiate with terrorists," said one man as he stepped forward.

Lady Justice grabbed him by the shirt and held him off his feet, shaking him as she spoke. "Terrorists? Who the hell are you calling terrorists? You attacked the city, you killed dozens of innocent citizens, you brutalized and bullied the people of this city, and you have the balls to call me a terrorist?" She tossed him to the ground where he landed on his butt. "Pray I never decide to terrorize you, my friend."

"We were following orders."

"Yeah, I've heard that shit before, when the cops killed my parents, when ..." The rage was threatening to take her over, but a small warrior in full armor with blue spirals on it, reached to lightly grip her arm. With a visible effort, Lady Justice regained control.

The man she'd thrown to the ground slowly regained his feet. "So, we have our volunteer. You're going outside the shield, my friend. Tell them to stand down and we'll negotiate the terms of release for these people. Remind them they've only seen our armor and our defenses.

"Tell them to back off and I'll stay inside the city. This is my city, I will bring justice to it, and I will defend it. Tell them that."

She waved her arm and a bright light appeared. She thrust him through it and another light appeared outside the shield. He stumbled out of the second light then both lights vanished. He was instantly surrounded by armed soldiers pointing weapons at him. The people still inside the shield watched as he was marched away.

Tasha turned back to the rest of the prisoners. "If your superiors place any value on your lives they'll back off enough to allow us to set you free, but know this, I won't hold you prisoner indefinitely. We don't have the resources to do that. Your ultimate fate is in the hands of your commanders."

"What if we want to join your army?" asked a voice.

Tasha turned and gazed at the man who's spoken. "We accept only veterans, men and women who have been used up and abandoned by the country they fought for. You're not qualified, yet.

"Intel."

"Yes Ma'am."

"Move them back beside the shield, with any luck we'll be able to let them go home."

Tasha started away, but Alicia and her cameraman were there, along with several others, all pointing microphones at her and babbling questions, pleading for a statement. With a snarl, she waved them to silence. "As you wish, I'll speak to the city."

She faced the cameras and began. "People of Georgia City, I've returned to bring justice to this town. There is now a shield over the city that can't be penetrated, those soldiers will not return. For now, the Soldiers of Justice, along with the city police, will maintain order. As soon as possible, that task will be fully turned over to the police, but they will remain under my watchful eye. Georgia City will never return to the bad old days of police brutality.

"Having said all that, this is what will happen. As soon as the army withdraws, the soldiers will be expelled. As well, any citizen who prefers to leave may do so. We'll hold none of you against your will. In addition, if you have family you wish to bring here, a system will be put in place to make that happen. For the moment I urge you to be patient while we get this situation sorted out."

As she finished speaking, Tasha blurred out of sight. She came down off combat mode at headquarters. With a deep sigh she sank into a chair and began wiping off the scary make-up. "What do you think, guys, too much?"

"Impressed the heck out of me," grinned Intel. "You do realize this will be a logistics nightmare."

"You mean figuring out who and how to let in or out, how to get food in that we can trust, what to do when they shut down the power grid and lay siege to the city, shit like that?"

"Yeah," he grinned, "shit like that."

"As commander of my army, that's your job to figure out," she sighed as she closed her eyes.

"Gee thanks, boss," he sighed. She chuckled softly, and he threw a balled-up paper at her. She batted it away without even opening her eyes.

Grinning, Kara settled down in the chair beside her. "You know, Tash honey, I think I have it figured out."

"Yeah? What's that?"

"The reason you're a bit shaky, the reasons Shadow put you in charge."

"Oh? Care to share?"

"Sure. First, this is your city, you spent time here establishing the persona of Lady Justice, you're familiar with the city, you have allies here, and the people of the city can relate a bit to you, like they do to Batman or Spiderman."

"Ah-huh. So, why not put you in charge, you're the famous Lady Blue."

"Because you're a natural leader, I'm not. Yes, I'm organized, and bossy ..."

"No argument here."

"Hush you," grinned Kara as she playfully slapped at Tasha's arm. "As I was saying, you're the natural leader. I get bogged down in the details too easy, you decide what needs to be done then appoint somebody to make it happen. You're a natural, and then there's the other."

"The other?"

"Honey, Seline will want to take North Bay back, and before she can do that she'll want Georgia City under control. Safe."

"Yeah? So why not North Bay First?"

"Not sure, but I'd say because we had so many more people in place for the take back. We have media people, high ranking police, and more. Tash, we operate differently here. We watch out for and support the people, her operations in North Bay were more focused on the big picture, going after the big bad, not controlling the city so much."

"So, it's like two completely different styles of operation. We're more like a police force, defenders, and she's more FBI sort of thing, more proactive against the big bosses."

"Yeah, something like that, at least that's my take on it. So, now it's up to you to change our world."

"Sure, no pressure. Help me?"

"By your side all the way, honey, right with you all the way."

The next morning Tasha was back in full war paint, wearing her microphone, and standing at the shield. It didn't take long for the general to appear facing her. "What do you want?" he bellowed over a bull horn.

"What do I want? I want your sorry ass in here to answer for the crimes these soldiers committed under your orders. I want your forces pulled back and the siege of my city lifted. I want to make an exchange."

"Exchange, what exchange do you propose?"

"You for your men. I've got over a hundred prisoners of war here, and I'll trade the lot for you."

The general was stunned, this was the last thing he'd expected. Lady Shadow just chuckled to herself. This was so typical of Tasha, she didn't ask for food, weapons, money, a means of escape, just the one man she wanted to bring to justice.

The general was caught in the trap and he knew it. There were cameras rolling on both sides of that shield, and he had no choice at all. He knew he was already dead, the great cop killer's reputation was clear, grab the guilty and break their neck, a swift and terrible justice.

If she had annihilated his troops instead of holding them captive, he'd have been on solid ground to go after her. Now she had him. If he refused the media would crucify him, and so would the court martial. Trembling in fear, he nodded his acquiescence.

"Command your troops to stand down and prepare to receive the hostages."

The general turned to the Major and nodded. A few barked orders later and all weapons had been lowered and the soldiers moved back. The general stood alone facing her through the shield. Tasha held up a remote and an archway appeared. She leaped through, seized the general and dragged him back behind the shield.

At a signal from her hand, her soldiers, all in full armor, began herding the captives through the archway. Once all were through she closed the doorway with her remote then turned and shoved the general at a tall red-haired alien woman. "This woman is the goddess Shadow, she will be asking the questions."

The general gulped, trembling in fear as the woman smiled at him, putting her gleaming fangs on display. She grabbed his collar then they both vanished.

THE HARD FACED MAN paced about his office, his personal guards standing silently by. Suddenly the phone rang, and he seized it up. "Smith?"

"Sir, General Slevin is gone."

"What? Explain."

"Sir, Lady Justice appeared to negotiate, but it went sideways instantly. She had only one demand, she offered to trade all her hostages for the general."

"She what?"

"That's what happened, Sir. We were expecting her to ask for food, medicine, money, amnesty, anything, but she just wanted the man who gave the original order to attack. The general agreed, the exchange was made, then Justice gave the general to Shadow. She called her a goddess. Shadow grabbed the general and they vanished."

The hard-faced man sank into the plush chair behind the desk and put his face in his hands for a moment. "Sir?"

"Come home, Smith, we've failed there, we must turn our efforts to damage control. Return to the office."

"Yes, Sir."

Hanging up the phone the man leaned back in his chair. He sighed heavily, then placed a call of his own. "Shadow is there with Justice, I suspected as much, but I'd hoped to finish them. Now she has Slevin."

"Understood," replied a cold voice, then the connection was broken.

MEANWHILE, BACK IN Georgia city.

"Boss?"

"I know, Intel, I know, but I wanted justice for the people of this city. That bastard is the man who gave the order that caused so many innocents to be killed. I wanted justice for them."

"The survivors would rather have food. Lady J, the city is running low on food and god knows what all else. We need to establish supply lines and fast."

"We will, Intel, we will."

"Got a plan you'd care to share?"

Tasha grinned at him. "Yep, I'm planning to turn pirate and my merry band of warriors will make that happen for me."

Intel grinned and shook his head. "Talk to me, Lady J."

"I've been playing with this portal gadget Shadow gave me. I can make a pretty big portal, but it doesn't last long. So, here's the plan. A few of us slip outside the city, hijack a food truck or two and zap them here."

"You knew that already, so it was safe to go after the general. Good one, Boss, that really took them off guard. I'm a bit surprised you didn't keep a few hostages back though."

"Just extra mouths to feed, Intel. We've got a city to feed and police, we don't have enough troops, we're spread pretty thin as it is. Can someone find Lenora and Lacy for me?"

Intel pointed at a soldier who saluted and hurried away. He returned shortly with Lady Warrior and the Seeker. "What's up, J?" asked Lacy as they arrived.

"The city needs supplies, Lacy, food would be the first order of business. Here's what I was thinking. You and your merry band of assassins slip outside, hijack a food truck, and send it here through a portal. Lennie, as a bounty hunter you've been all over the place. I need you to locate the trucks for Lacy to steal."

"Seriously? Lady Justice wants me to steal truckloads of food?"

"Yes, I want you to confiscate the food we need, take it from the country that attacked us. That's only just, right?"

Lenora laughed with delight. "Oh yes, my sister, that is indeed just. I know exactly where we can find what we need. There's a gigantic warehouse out near Cooperstown, it's owned by a big food chain. We can catch full trucks coming out and zap 'em right here. Sounds like fun. Gather your gang, Lacy. Let's go."

Car Thieves

"**C**hosen, mount up," shouted Ryder as she leaped onto her flyer, as she called them. The others mounted and started their machines. "Ready Ellen." Ellen held out her arm and a shining portal of light appeared. Like a silent tide the riders of the Chosen swept through at speed, the portal vanishing behind them.

They appeared on the open highway. "So, where the hell are we?" asked Thunder.

"Road to Seattle by the looks of it," replied Marla.

"Yep, that's where're supposed to be," said Ryder.

"Mickey's bar?" asked Thunder.

"Mickey's bar," replied Ryder. "We need to find a car thief." They sped away with Thunder in the lead. They rolled in to town on the near silent speeders, drawing lots of attention. They parked in front of the bar and strode inside.

"Holy shit, it's the Chosen," exclaimed the old bartender as he saw Thunder enter. "Jesus, Thunder, we heard all you guys were dead. They showed the bombed out garage on TV. How the hell did you get away?"

"We got lucky and a new job, beer all round and one ginger ale."

"Whaddya mean, job? Since when to the Chosen work for wages?" he asked as he started drawing the beer.

"We don't," replied Thunder. "We used to work for the Fallen Angel, Ryder took over from the Angel, and a few days ago she signed us on with Lady Shadow."

"Lady Shadow? That tabloid freak, the alien with a dragon from back east? Seriously, that's your story?"

"That's our story."

"You're serious, aren't you? You're really serious? The alien is real?"

"Lady Shadow is a goddess," said Ryder as she picked up a chair with a huge man sitting on it, gently depositing chair and man on the bar. "Keep respect in your voice when you speak her name." She took the ginger ale and walked away.

Both Mickey and the man on the chair were dumbfounded. Mickey shook it off first. "Go on you, get the hell down offa there." Carefully the man climbed down and retrieved his chair. "Thunder, who or what the hell is that kid?"

"That kid is Ryder, the Fallen Angel's younger sister. It's a bad idea to piss her off."

"I can see that. So, this Shadow is real, and you guys ride for her now? How did that happen?"

"Things were quiet, and we were just hanging out at the garage when Shadow stepped out of the wall. Ryder knew who it was and ordered us back. She dropped to one knee and pledged us to work for Shadow, asked for orders. Lady Shadow only said one word I could hear. Run.

"We ran. Shadow disappeared and Ryder was bawling for us to mount up. We burned out of there just as the shelling started. Just made it. We put the hammer down, but they were using choppers and it looked bad, then Lady Shadow appeared and made a ball of light. Ryder gunned it into the light and we followed.

"Lady saves your ass, gives you new and better rides, you make it happen when she needs something."

"Ah-huh. So, what does she need?"

"Right now we're looking for a chop shop, the Lady wants a new car. Freddy still in business?" The old bartender nodded, and Thunder grinned as he took his beer and started to walk away. "Good to know."

Mickey called him back. "Thunder, can I ask a question?"

The tall biker turned back, a frown clouding his face. "You're being awful damned nosy, Mick. What's on your mind?"

"What the hell is that over there? The big thing sitting with Kyle and Marla?"

"That's Dex, he's a member of the Chosen. You don't need to know any more than that."

"So this is the part where I shut up and forget you were ever here?"

"That would be it." The man just nodded, and Thunder walked away to sit with Ryder and two others. "Nosy old bugger. Did he hit the panic button?"

Ryder chuckled. "Nope. He's curious as hell but playing fair. You get what we need?"

"Yeah, Freddy's still there. He'll want a lot of money, Ryder."

"I'll see if he's willing to take a trade."

"Trade. What'll you offer him in trade?"

"His life."

"That should do it," grinned Thunder. "He'll have a lot of firepower in that garage with him. Never take your eyes of him."

"I won't. Finish that yak piss now and we'll be on our way."

"It's called beer, Ryder," grinned the woman at the table.

"Tastes like yak piss," grumbled Ryder.

"And just how would you know that?"

"You'd be amazed at some of the things I've been forced to put in my mouth."

The woman's grin faded instantly. She knew Ryder had been a child sex slave before the Fallen Angel rescued her. "Jesus, Ryder, I'm sorry ..."

Ryder sighed and patted her hand. "Forget it. That time of the month, I'm just cranky."

"You've been hanging out with the Angel for days," grinned Thunder. "That's what's got you going."

Ryder laughed. "Yeah, maybe. Come on, let's go find a car thief." If anybody heard what she said, they kept it to themselves. The Chosen had always been extremely dangerous, but there was something even more dangerous about them now. Everyone just sighed with relief as they walked out.

They moved quietly through town, drawing lots of attention. Curious people tried to see what or where the machines met the ground, but all they could see was air. Bemused, they watched as the hard-bitten riders moved down the street.

Thunder led them to a run-down area of town where they parked in front of an old warehouse. It was all locked up, but there were cars outside, nice looking cars. Ryder tried the office door, but it was locked. "Come on, open up," she shouted, but got no answer.

She waved her arm and the Chosen spread out, surrounding the building. A moment later she spun around and lashed out with her foot. The office door exploded inward. Several shots rang out, but Ryder had already darted aside. She was grinning. "Hey in there, is this the customer service entrance?"

More shots were fired then a voice. "Get the hell away from here. We don't want nothin' to do with the Chosen."

"Too bad for you, Buttercup, we have business for you. You can either settle down and negotiate like reasonable men, or we'll have to do this the hard way."

"Fuck you, bitch." More gunfire followed the voice.

"Hard-headed bugger, isn't he?" grinned Ryder. "Thunder, Kyle, Marla, armor up. Let's go have some face time with these guys."

All three popped up their armor as did Ryder. She walked through the office door followed by her three friends. They ignored the bullets bouncing off their armor as they spread out through the shop, disarming the men they cornered there. When all were disarmed, Ryder dropped her armor. "Okay now, which one of you up-standing citizens of this fair city is Freddy?"

"That would be this sniveling piece of crap," growled Thunder as he thrust a small man towards Ryder. The Chosen lowered their armor.

"Well then, Freddy, I'm Ryder, and I lead this merry band of free riding souls. We came here to do business, but you weren't very welcoming. I'm extremely disappointed in you."

"What do you want?" he asked, as he leaned as far from her as Thunder's grip on his collar would allow.

"A friend of ours wrecked his car a few days ago. He's somewhat of a celebrity, so maybe you've heard of him. His name's Viper." The man swallowed hard at that, he recognized the name and knew the reputation.

"Okay, so you want a viper. Why come to me?"

"We were in the neighborhood, asked around, and you were recommended. How about it, Freddy, can you get us a car? No stock junk now, I want something special for my buddy, something that'll move in a hurry, if you know what I mean."

"No. No way in hell."

"Wow, Freddy, that sounds like you know where the perfect car is, but it makes you nervous." He didn't respond, nor would he make eye contact. "Okay, Freddy, tell you what. I'm in a good mood today, so you tell me where to find this car and I'll steal it myself."

"I can't, he'll kill me if he even thinks I put you on to his car. Please, you don't want to do this. He's the head of an Asian gang. You have no idea what they're capable of."

"Aw shit," sighed Thunder. "Ryder ..."

"She rode with us, Thunder. She was Chosen. You know what we have to do."

"Yeah, you're right. Kyle, warn the others. We're going to give this armor a real test."

"We doing this for Mai, Ryder?"

"Yes, we are, Kyle."

"Good. I liked that gal."

"So did we all, brother," said Ryder. "Get the others ready, we'll head out as soon as Freddy tells us where to find the car."

"Look, I told you, it's worth my life to ..." He got no further before Ryder grabbed him and slammed him hard against the wall.

"Listen carefully, asshole. Your life's already on the line here. Those bastards killed our sister, and I intend to visit a little justice on them before this day is through. Yes, I need that car, but the Asian gang is a real bonus, so here's the deal. Tell me what I want to know, or I'll fire up that welding torch and start warming up your balls. Understand?"

"Please ..."

"Where?"

"I can't ..."

"Thunder, bring me that torch, would you?" Suddenly the man in her grasp wet himself and began to weep, babbling out the address. "Got that Thunder?"

"Got it. I know where that is."

Ryder tossed aside her victim. "Let's ride. Oh, Freddy, if you try to warn those bastards, I'll come back here, and you won't like it. Let's go, guys." There was a soft swishing sound as thirty speeders swept away from the building.

A short time later the Chosen sat gazing at the tall office building. "How do you want to do this, Ryder?" asked Thunder.

"The hard way. We armor up, kick down the door and get messy. This one's for Mai."

"Works for me," grinned Kyle.

Dex worked his way closer to them. "Lady Ryder, are the Chosen going to attack that building?"

"Absolutely."

"Please, I ..."

"Easy brother," she replied as she gripped his arm lightly. "This is aggressive, and I know how you feel about that and why. I won't ask you to attack another, your job is to stay back and protect the bikes. That work for you?"

"gargjsl kewrxs ..." he slapped at the unit on his jacket. "Thank you, Ryder. Yes, I can do that for you."

Ryder chuckled and squeezed his arm. "Dex, you really do have to get a new one of those things."

They swept into the underground secure parking lot, going in the wrong way, crashing through the barrier, and floating safely above the spiked strips designed to flatten tires. Security alarms began to sound and armed men came running to open fire on the armored invaders. It did them no good at all.

The Chosen waded through the armed men, destroying all in their path. Methodically, floor by floor, they advanced until they reached the executive offices on the top floor. Finally, only one man was left facing them. A man in his fifties, wearing an expensive suit and holding a sword, waited dispassionately as Ryder kicked in his office door and leaped through. "Are you the man in charge here?"

"I am."

"All yours, Kyle."

As the huge armored figure approached the man leaped, lashing out with sword, it shattered against the armor. He threw the broken sword aside and leaped at Kyle, striking at him with his foot. The blow staggered the big man, but he didn't fall. He shook it off and chuckled, then advanced again. A series of kicks and blows rained down on the armored figure, but he shook them all off and kept coming. A gun appeared from the suit jacket, but the bullets struck the armor and fell to the floor.

"Kyle, quit screwing around and get this done. We've got someplace to be."

"Yes Ma'am."

The man in the suit stopped fighting then and dropped his gun, glaring at the huge figure. Kyle struck him a blow on the shoulder spinning him around. Powerful arms encircled the man's neck. "Her name was Mai. You bastards killed her father, forced her mother into prostitution, then you killed her. She was one of us, she was ours. For these crimes against the Chosen, you die."

Those huge arms jerked, there was a snapping sound, and the man in the suit melted to the floor, dead. "Justice is served."

Ryder chuckled at that. "Tasha would be proud of that one, Kyle. Come on, we have a car to steal."

"Right behind you, sister."

They found the car in the executive parking slot. The keys were in the lot office and they were soon inside. "Okay, so who's driving this rig and how do we get the extra bike back, they're DNA activated." asked Ryder.

"Lisa can drive it," said one of the bikers. "She rides behind me anyway, so no bike gets left behind."

"Works for me," grinned Ryder as the slim girl in Chosen colors slid behind the wheel.

"Wow, this is some car. Jeez, Jimmy, maybe I'll trade you in for Viper."

"Women can be so damn fickle," laughed the biker as he squeezed her arm and walked away. She grinned, closed the car door, and started the engine.

Outside they found a police blockade, cars sideways across the exit, and plenty of guns aimed at their direction. A voice began barking orders at them over the bullhorn, but they ignored it. Ryder dismounted and walked toward the barricade. The voice became more insistent as she neared, but she continued to pay it no heed.

As she drew closer they opened fire and were once again ignored. While bullets fell to the ground or bounced away, Ryder seized the front of one police car and lifted it up, dragged it out of the way, then waved the Chosen by. The armored riders began to speed past the police, then a big engine screamed. A jet black viper shot out of the parking area and flashed away, followed by the rest of the Chosen.

Out on the highway they encountered police pursuit. Ryder sped on ahead then spun to a stop, waved her arm, and created a shining portal. The Chosen parted, and the viper raced past heading straight for the ball of light in the road. The car vanished through the portal, followed swiftly by the Chosen. Ryder was the last through then the portal vanished.

"WELL, WHAT DO YOU THINK, Vic? Will this do?" asked Ryder as he sat in the car, checking it out.

"Oh yeah, this is a lot more car than I had before. This is awesome, Ryder. Did you steal it?"

"Yup, we took it off a crime boss, a guy who was running an Asian gang."

"What about his gang?"

"We sort of had to go through them to get to him. We had issues with this guy for past offences. We settled our debt and brought you a new car as requested."

Victor laughed. "Ryder, you rock. Well done, girl. Shadow will be proud."

"Before you use this vehicle, I want to make some modifications to it," said Dex.

"Modifications?"

"Yes, I'd like to exchange the propulsion unit for one like the speeders use, plus I want to add defensive shields."

"Shields and faster?"

"Yes. Quieter as well, and not so stinky."

"She's all yours, Dex, my friend," said Vic as he got back out of the car. "Need any help?"

"Thank you, no, apparently I already have an apprentice."

"You do?"

"I do. Kyle, would you take this infernal machine to the repair shop please?"

"On it, Boss," grinned Kyle.

"Kyle?" asked Ryder.

"How else am I going to learn how to fix the speeders, Ryder. Dex says he'll teach me, so I signed on."

"Have fun with that," she grinned.

Two days later they brought the car back to the barracks. Victor crashed three times before he got the hang of the car's new abilities. Fortunately, his armor protected him, and the car's new shields protected it. The Viper was ready for action once again.

The next day they went through the portal into Georgia city. The Viper had arrived, and within hours every gang member in the city was aware of it and in hiding. And then there was the arrival of that bike gang, the Chosen. For some reason, Viper seemed to like them, so did Lady Justice.

On the Hunt

While the girls were trying to restore order to a city of a million people, a sleek Mercedes slipped out through the shield with two women aboard. Seline Elmore, aka Lady Shadow, was driving, a well-tanned woman with platinum blonde hair was relaxing in the passenger's seat. "Looks like we're away clear, sweetie. Nobody's following us."

"Great. I figured all the attention would be at the park side highway, what with Viper and the Chosen showing up."

"Yes indeed," grinned Ellen. "It's all in the timing. So, where are we going?"

"Washington. The director of the CIA has to know who's behind this, if it isn't him, and I'm not so sure it isn't."

"So, planning to take him off world again?"

"Bet your boots I am. This man has information and I want it. Want to come with me?"

"Love to."

"Dex give you armor?"

"He did. Got my little remote right here."

"Awesome. I ..." her phone was ringing. "Seline Elmore."

"Seline, it's Miranda. Where are you?"

"On my way to Washington, a few hours away. Tell me everything is under control there."

"Oh yeah, we're good. Tasha's getting everybody put to work, getting things organized. No, it's you I'm concerned about."

"What is it Lady Watcher?"

"I thought you might be heading that way. Seline, the darkness is growing there, pulling back its forces. I believe they're expecting a retaliatory strike. They'll be watching for you. Please be extremely careful."

"I am duly warned, Lady Watcher."

"Do you want the sisters to join you there."

"No, I've got this. Keep an eye on us, and if I call, send the troops."

"Will do." The connection broke and Seline dropped her phone back on the dash.

"That doesn't sound hopeful," sighed Ellen. "What do you want to do, go back for the girls, do a hit and run?"

"No love, I plan to play dirty. These guys will be expecting a major strike at the government. That's what they'd do, that's what any country that was attacked would do, strike at the government or military targets. I'm Lady Shadow ... something different from anything they've ever encountered before."

"You mean a goddess."

"Please don't call me that. It's all bad enough the rest of them do it. I'm just a girl with a special skill set and a wild imagination."

"You're my love, my reason to exist, and my girlfriend," smiled Ellen. "So, girlfriend, how do we go at these guys?"

"We hit 'em where and how they would never expect in a million years. We're neutrals, and they've never had to deal with that. They'll be expecting me to retaliate, to try to defeat them, but defeating the dark isn't what we're trying to do, we're just trying to push it back to restore some balance. Now, here's what I want to do ..."

As the big car rolled along the highway, Ellen's grin of delight grew wider and wider. Those men would never see this coming. She had only one question. "Honey, I love it, but can you do it?"

"Easily."

"All illusion?"

"Not this time. I'm not playing with these guys anymore, this one's going to be real. They established the rules of the game themselves."

Ellen nodded, but didn't speak, she just reached for and gently squeezed Seline's hand. Seline may not like the title of goddess, but what else could she be called? This latest attack on them had caused Seline to cast off her fears and become what she truly was. That both frightened and drew Ellen. Like it or not, Ellen Cameron's girlfriend was a goddess, and she was getting angry.

They pulled into the hotel parking lot by midafternoon, and Ellen went in as herself to check them in. Once they were in the room, Seline morphed into Lady Shadow. "Are you ready, Ellen my love?"

Ellen morphed into the platinum blonde. "Ready."

THE HARRIED YOUNG MAN strode purposely down the corridor. As he neared a door two security guards stepped into his path. "I have urgent news for the Chiefs of Staff," he declared, showing his ID. The guards stepped aside, and one opened the door for him.

He stepped through and screamed as he stepped into empty space. His flailing arm managed to grab the door sill as he fell. The two guards stood staring dumbfounded into the misty emptiness where a room full of the nations top leaders should have been.

"Help me," begged a voice from the floor, and the guards hauled the young man back to the corridor. "What the hell is going on here?"

"No idea at all," replied one guard while the other called for assistance. They stood gazing at the empty space where the war room should have been, while reinforcements came pounding up the hallway.

IN THE MEETING ROOM one man stood pacing, rambling on and on about something that wasn't making a lot of sense to the others in the room. One admiral glanced at his watch and muttered to himself. "Where the hell is that man? He should have been here by now."

He stood and went to the door, swinging it wide then screamed in fear as he fell through, clinging to the doorknob. Two others rushed to him and pulled him back inside. "Sweet baby Jesus," hissed a general as he gazed out the open door. Outside was a mist above a roiling sea below. Wave after wave crashed against a slender pillar of stone that was holding up the meeting room.

"Impressive, isn't it?" asked a woman's voice. Every man spun about to see a woman sitting in the president's chair. She was finger combing her platinum hair and smiling. "Sit down, gentlemen, and I'll explain what's happening to you."

"That's my chair," said the man who'd been speaking earlier.

"Go sit down," she commanded as she pointed at an empty chair and glared at him. Shrinking away from her, he sat where indicated. "Now then, gentlemen, there is someone who wishes to speak with you. She has removed this room to another world, to avoid distractions from security guards and the like.

"My name is Meda, short for Mediator. I'm here to keep things civil between you and the Lady of Shadows. She will obey me, will you?"

"This is preposterous, I ..."

"Be silent," commanded Meda. "From this moment forward you, sir, will speak only when spoken to, or you will be removed from this meeting. If you bother to look through that door you will understand that there is nowhere for you to go. This planet has only three mountains that rise above the waters. The others are far from this place. I strongly suggest you shut the hell up.

"Now, gentlemen, are we agreed? Will you accept me as mediator?"

"What happens if we don't?"

"I leave you here and return home. Lady Shadow will wait until others have been appointed to your positions, then she will bring them here. So, I ask you again, and for the last time, do you accept the terms of my service?"

"We have no choice, do we," growled a general. "We accept. So, what happens now?"

"Now we await Lady Shadow and hear her complaint. Ah, here she comes now." They spun to look where she was pointing. Against the far wall the shaded areas were coalescing.

A shadow darkened and took form. A tall woman in gore bespattered armor, wearing her red hair in a thick braid thrown across her shoulder, strode into the room. Her ears were delicate and up-swept, her canine teeth extended as gleaming fangs, and her fierce green eyes burned with a tightly controlled fury.

"Welcome, Lady Shadow."

"I greet you, Great Meda. I beg permission to have Minx join us today."

The blonde inclined her head. "Granted."

Shadow tossed her staff on the table and it morphed into a huge cobra that reared up and flared its hood with a hiss. All the men gasped and pulled away from the table.

Meda chuckled and leaned forward in her chair. "Gentlemen, this is Minx, a lie detector of sorts. You see, he hates it when someone lies to Lady Shadow, and he always knows. His bite is fatal, so I strongly suggest you don't test him.

"Now, gentlemen, place your hands on the table and we will begin." No one moved, so she leaned forward again. "Unless you wish to spend the rest of your life in this room on an alien planet, I suggest you comply." Reluctantly, they put their hands on the table. "You may begin, Lady Shadow."

Shadow began to pace about, obviously struggling to get control of her emotions. Finally, she stopped and faced the men gathered about the table.

"A number of days ago a military strike was executed against three separate points within your country. Each strike was swift and deadly, designed to destroy me and my sisters as well as those humans close to us. Artillery, plus rocket fire, and other heavy weapons as well as ground troops were used. Those attacks failed to achieve their purpose, but there was a great loss of life among the citizens of Georgia City and North Bay.

"Be it known to you that Lady Justice has reclaimed Georgia City. Once she has secured that city she will surely begin to look for whoever ordered these attacks, however, that is no concern of mine." That statement sent most of them into shock. If that wasn't her issue, then what was?

"Now then, who can tell me anything about the Brotherhood?"

Startled by her question, they looked at each other, but none spoke. One admiral looked discomfited. Shadow rounded on him instantly. "Tell me what you know of the Brotherhood."

The man swallowed hard, but Meda intervened. "Forgive me, Lady Shadow, but by the terms of engagement, you may ask questions only, not make demands until we get to the mediation part of the agenda.

Shadow nodded, "my apologies," and began to pace about the room. Finally, she turned to the admiral again. "Are you indeed a member of the Brotherhood?" He gulped and nodded. "Did the Brotherhood order these attacks upon me and my people?" Again, the man nodded.

Still pacing, ordering her thoughts, Shadow opened and closed her fists slowly as she fought for control. She turned back to the Admiral. "What is the Brotherhood?"

He swallowed hard before choking out an answer. "A very old secret society."

"What is its purpose?"

"Complete world domination," he stammered.

"Are there any other members of this organization in this room at this time?"

His eyes bugged out as he fought for breath. A trembling hand reached for and loosened his tie. "You will answer the question," commanded Meda.

His eyes darted to two others then he choked out a single word. "No." The snake struck instantly, fastening its fangs deeply into his neck. He screamed and fought, but the beast held tightly to him. As he fell from the chair Lady Shadow reached for and retrieved the cobra which was now a staff once again.

"That hurts, doesn't it," she grinned, exposing her gleaming fangs. "This is the antidote," she said as she tossed a small vial to the man writhing on the floor. "Drink it all, every drop. Quickly now, for your eyes grow dim even as we speak."

He did. With trembling hands, he pulled the stopper from the bottle and held it above his mouth, gulping down the precious liquid. "You'll survive, for now. I do urge you gentlemen not to test Minx again, for that was the last of the antidote that I brought with me."

She turned to a man in an expensive suit. "Are you a member of the Brotherhood?"

"Yes." His eyes were wide and his voice shaky as he eyed the huge snake. It was watching him closely.

"Why were my people attacked?"

"You are considered a threat to the Brotherhood."

"Did you order that attack?"

"No."

"Who did?"

"I don't know."

Lady Shadow looked at the snake, but it hadn't moved. She nodded, thoughtfully. "Who controls the Brotherhood in this country?"

"I don't know." Again, the snake made no move.

Shadow pursed her lips and thought for a moment. "Who in the Brotherhood do you answer to?"

"Mr. Kaufman."

"Do you believe he answers to another in this country?"

"Yes."

"As do I," muttered Shadow. She rounded on the director of the CIA. "Were you aware this attack would happen?"

"No."

"Do you know who ordered it?"

"No."

"Do you know the current whereabouts of Mr. Kaufman?"

"No, I assumed you took him."

"I took one, it's the brother I want now."

"I have no idea where he is." The snake still hadn't moved.

"All right, I believe I shall get no further useful information here. Let us move on to the negotiations. I expect you all to bargain in good faith. For those of you who do not, be aware, Minx is still watching.

"These are my demands." She waved her arm and a map of Georgia City and surrounding area appeared on one wall. "This city and a ten-mile buffer zone are controlled by my people at this moment. You will make no attempt to interfere with them, for all intents and purposes this area is a foreign country. You will accept that you have no authority there. Will you agree to this?"

The man who'd been speaking as Meda first entered the room shouted. "No bloody way in hell we'll ..." he screamed and leaped back, falling to the floor as the snake struck. Fortunately for him, Lady Shadow had reached out and caught the snake, changing it back to a staff.

"You prefer the alternative?" asked Shadow.

"What's the alternative?" asked another man.

"All out war with me," replied Shadow, her voice so cold everyone shrank from her. "You have no weapons that can penetrate my shields, my armor, and you have yet to see the weapons I can bring to bear against you.

"I'm offering you a peace treaty, you will never attack me again, and I won't attack you. I will, however, pursue my vendetta against the Brotherhood, both within your country and abroad. I will also take back North Bay including a ten-mile buffer. Agree to these terms and we can live in peace, our citizens trading freely back and forth as before, only now my people will maintain order and govern within the afore mentioned zones.

"What say you?"

Meda leaned her elbows on the table and smiled. "Gentlemen, I suggest you agree to Lady Shadow's terms. All things considered, it seems more than reasonable."

"It does," said the director of the CIA. "I say we agree to it."

Several others agreed as well, but the man on the floor refused. Shadow walked over to squat down near him and gaze into his eyes. "You actually prefer the alternative? You'd rather sacrifice the lives of your entire military as well as half the population of your nation in a vain attempt to stop me? Is your ego so fragile that you can't admit when you're wrong, that you're beaten?

"You lost all control of your people, your government, you stood by while they attacked the citizens of your own cities, and now you want to thrust your nation into a war you cannot hope to survive? You amaze me and make me regret stopping the snake's attack.

"I suggest you listen to your aides here. I'll give you a few moments to think it over. Gentlemen, you may confer with your leader." She walked to the far side of the huge room.

It took a while, but eventually, Meda called her back. "Lady Shadow, these men appear to have reached a consensus."

Shadow returned and tossed her staff on the table once again. The snake reared up and flicked its tongue. "Minx, be kind enough to point out any man who bargains in bad faith."

With poor grace the man rose and spoke. "We agree to your terms."

"Then you will withdraw all military forces from my borders immediately upon your return, agreed?"

"Agreed," he replied sullenly.

"I have already dealt with the general who ordered the strike against me. It was his commander that I wanted. I shall assume that Mr. Kaufman is that man and proceed from there. Have a nice day, gentlemen. Lady Meda, shall I escort you home?"

"Thank you, Lady Shadow. Gentlemen, I can assure you from a position of experience, it would be a serious mistake to renege on the agreement with Lady Shadow. She's not of a forgiving nature."

"Come, Meda, let us away," said Shadow as she seized the snake, turning it back into a staff. As Meda touched her arm, both she and Lady Shadow vanished from the room.

A general watched out the open doorway as the mist rose up to block his view, and then he was gazing out into a hallway full of security officers with drawn weapons.

Later that day, while security people and dozens of scientists were going over the building, especially the meeting room, a general sat at his desk, the door locked, and speaking to the face on his computer.

"No Sir, we dare not attack her again. What, no, the others won't do it, nor will I. In her own words, we can't penetrate her defenses, and we haven't seen the weapons she has access to. Sir, I did notice one thing of great interest that she said. She said she'd taken your brother, she didn't say she'd killed him. I believe Mr. Kaufman might still be alive."

Back at the hallway, the confused men were still trying to figure out what happened. "I'm thinking it was all illusion," said one of the men who'd been there.

"It was no illusion," said another. "Look." He pulled back his collar and showed them the marks where the cobra had bitten him. "No, this was no illusion. People, for some unknown reason one of our generals went off the deep end and attacked a god."

"A god? Is that what you think that alien is?"

"Compared to us, that's exactly what she is. We got lucky. Did you notice she didn't seem to want revenge? She's after somebody else, and we damn near got in her way. We fuck up again and this whole country could end up as collateral damage. No, gentlemen, our task now is to keep our fearless leader from doing something stupid and getting us all killed."

"Second that," muttered another.

Return to North Bay

The female soldier in full armor saluted and waved them through as the big car rolled easily past the archway and into Georgia City with Ellen at the wheel, Seline asleep with her head in Ellen's lap. She drove up to headquarters then parked and gently shook Seline's shoulder.

"Are we there yet?"

Ellen giggled at that. "Yes, honey, we're here. Let's go in and report to the kids now. How are you feeling?"

"Way better than I usually do."

"Oh? All right you, what aren't you telling me?"

"When Moragah gave me the warning and told me to become what I am, she stripped away all the stops, all the things that sort of helped me stay in check."

"Such as?"

"Using the juice doesn't tire me anymore like it did. I just love napping with my head in your lap."

"Brat," laughed Ellen. "Come on, let's go in."

"Seline," shouted Miranda as she grabbed Lady Shadow in a bear hug and swung her around.

Shrieking with laughter Seline returned the hug. "Put me down, you savage. Well, it looks like things here are under control. Go find Tasha now so we can report in."

"I'll call all the sisters," said Miranda as she turned back to the house and whipped out her phone.

Miranda called a full meeting of the inner circle, the sisters, Viper, Intel, and Decoy were there as well. Ellen gave them a full report. "So, we're a separate country now?" asked Intel. "How is that supposed to work?"

"Just like it's doing now," replied Seline as she morphed into Lady Shadow. "Tasha will rule here, and I will return to North Bay, unless you all believe it would be best if I stay here for a time."

"I think that's your decision to make," said Lady Justice.

"Do you need me here, Tasha?"

"No, I think we've got it under control. You need to reclaim North Bay. You'll want Miranda, Lacy, and Penny with you as well as Viper and his new hot rod. You'll probably want Decoy and his troops also. I would like to keep Ryder and the Chosen for a while though, we'll be a bit short handed."

"It shall be as you require, my sister. Is there anything else you need?"

"The general who ordered the attack, is he still alive?"

"He is."

"I want him."

Tasha had gone so cold the others all shivered. Lady Shadow vanished, then a few moments later she returned with a disheveled General Slevin held by the collar. Lady Shadow thrust the hapless man towards Tasha.

He took one look at the cold-eyed warrior and tried to run. She had him in a heartbeat. Powerful arms encircled his neck and a cold voice spoke at his ear. "For the countless murders of Georgia City citizens, you now forfeit your miserable life."

Her arms tightened, there was a snapping sound, and he went limp. She tossed the body toward the door. "Justice is served."

As she turned back to the room she saw Alicia with her phone in her hand. "Allie, what did you just do?"

"I filmed the execution of the general. Can I use it J, I think the people of the city would like to see that you mean business?"

Tasha gazed at her for a moment then grinned. "But I wasn't wearing my war paint."

Alicia smiled at her friend as she relaxed her shoulders. "I really don't think you need it anymore, Tash."

"I suppose not. Okay, you can use it, but that's all, none of the other stuff that went on here."

"I'll put it on my computer and edit it right now. You can okay it, or not, before I send it to air, deal?"

"Deal. Okay folks, I guess that's it. Ryder, I need you guys to help Intel and the chief of police keep order until a new police force can be trained."

"Well, that does sort of go against the grain," grinned Ryder, "but we'll do our best."

Tasha laughed and gave her a gentle hug. "Just don't let Kyle give Kara too much beer."

"Actually, before we get in a hurry," said Penny, "shouldn't we discuss this a bit further? You're the boss, Lady Shadow, you say go, then we go, I just think ..."

Lady Shadow had pulled Penny into a gentle hug. "Getting in a hurry, was I, Penny? What did I miss?"

Penny returned the hug then stepped back a bit. "Well, it's just that we're still spread pretty thin here as is."

"She's right," agreed Ellen. "If we spread ourselves too thin we're wide open for a fresh attack. Okay, we've shut down the chances of a major attack like the last one, but who knows what might come at us next? The Brotherhood isn't going to take this lying down. Next could be disguised snipers, assassins, organized crime soldiers, or god knows what else."

Lady Shadow smiled and squeezed Ellen's hand. "All right, you two put those analytical minds together and devise us a course of action."

Penny grinned and winked at Ellen. "What do you think? Should Lady Blue go poke around North Bay for a while and see what's on the go?"

"I don't like the idea of you going in there alone, Penny," said Shadow.

"Understood, but, in all modesty, of the lot of us, I have the most experience at crawling around the underbelly of strange cities. Lenora can keep an eye on me from here, so you'll know instantly if it goes sideways on me."

"Want company?" asked Lacy.

"Warrior, you'll just start a fight and get me in trouble with the boss."

"Was that a yes?"

Penny laughed at that. "Sure, Lacy. You and I work well together, let's go poke around and see what's what in North Bay."

THEY'D BEEN ON THE road for two hours with Lacy driving. "Want me to take a turn at the wheel?" asked Penny.

"Sure, I'll stop so we can switch. Be careful, the damn thing pulls to the right. I just hope it'll last to get us to North Bay. Don't know why Shadow didn't give us a ride through a portal anyway."

"Because we need to see what's going on outside Georgia City as well as North Bay. Lacy, why the big pout?"

Lacy burst out laughing. "Okay, I miss my damn truck, okay? If we were in a decent ride I'd enjoy the drive. So why the hell did you steal this old wreck anyway, is that just a habit?"

Penny chuckled. "You know, I think it is. I'm so used to keeping a low profile as Lady Blue, that I just grabbed it out of habit, and I didn't steal it, it was one of four the guys took away from a street gang. They probably stole it."

"Okay, fair enough. Penny, how are you doing?"

"You mean without Moragah?"

"Yeah, that."

"It's hard, Lacy. I feel like a big part of me, the best part of me, got ripped away. Don't get me wrong, I love Seline, I do, and I'll happily do whatever she asks of me, but she can't fill that hole inside."

"I know what you mean. I wonder though, is it because she can't, or she hasn't thought to try yet."

"Don't know, girl, but ... what the hell is that?"

"Where?"

Penny pulled over. "There, up ahead and to the right."

"I have no idea," said Lacy as she shifted onto warrior more, "but I'd really like to have a look."

"With you all the way, Lady Warrior." Penny pulled the car off the road completely then they got out and shifted onto combat mode. A short run at super speed later they were inside a stand of trees looking out at a military camp.

"How close to North Bay do you think we are?" asked Lacy.

"Close, but well out of sight," mused Penny. "I don't like this at all. Let's wait until dark then take a closer look." Lacy nodded her agreement then settled to the ground and closed her eyes. Penny grinned and joined her.

The sun was low in the sky when they moved in closer to have a look. What they saw surprised and disgusted them. Penny struggled to hold Lacy in check. "Hush, dammit, Lacy, stop it, we're not supposed to be here. Come on, get a grip."

"Fuck it, Penny, we can take 'em. They already know everybody's back on Earth, they must know we took back Georgia City. This is bullshit. We can stop this."

"Come on, super woman, use your head. Think, what's going on here?"

"They're looting the city and holding a big flea market. Dirty bastards."

"More, Lacy, tell me more. What else do you see?"

With a visible effort Lady Warrior got control of the rage and took a closer look. "Too many guards, heavy weapons, ... trap?"

"Trap. Shadow worked a deal to pull them back out of the cities, and we already had the shield in place, so North Bay was their only target left. When they pulled out they looted the place then set this up, trying to lure one or more of us outside the buffer zone."

"Yeah, I'll bet you're right about that, Penny, but why would they? Justice had already taken the general out of the picture. Who the hell is continuing the vendetta?"

"Don't know, but I'd like to find out. Want to sneak in for a closer look then make a run for North Bay?"

"Let's do it."

They shifted on to combat mode and easily passed by the guards. Those soldiers stood wondering about the sudden blast of wind but saw nothing. Penny and Lacy crouched behind a large truck, listening to the man on the phone in a nearby tent.

"No sir, no sign of any of them yet. Yes, sir, I'll keep up the pressure until ordered to move out. Yes sir, I have everyone on full alert, none of those freaks will get near this tent alive. The captives are secure. Yes sir, I will. Power to the Brotherhood."

Penny put her lips right beside Lacy's ear and whispered softly. "Want to see who they've got captive in there?"

Lacy turned her head to whisper in Penny's ear. "You say the sweetest things." Penny snickered and moved closer to the tent holding the captives.

Inside the tent the major was taunting the captives. "You know, I just don't get it. Why the hell haven't those super freaks come to rescue you two. I mean, your daughter is some sort of visionary, right? A super psychic? How come she didn't see this coming? Why hasn't she come for you? If she's such a super hero, why isn't she here trying to save her own mother?

"And you, your girlfriend is that killer bounty hunter, why hasn't she come to save her favorite cop? Huh? You guys break up before the war or something? Well, super cop, say something."

"You're an asshole," replied a male voice.

That remark was followed by the sound of a fist striking a body. Lacy started forward, but Penny held her back. Lacy pulled her close and whispered. "Dammit, Penny ..."

"We'll get them out, Lacy, but we can't let them know who did it. We need to make it look like they escaped on their own. Look, they're expecting super powered people coming in, so all eyes are facing outward. We take that guy down from behind then find a fast way out of here."

"And there it is," breathed Lacy.

"What???"

"My truck. The bastards stole my stolen truck. It's right there and the path is clear. If the keys are in it, then that's our way out. Be right back."

Penny held her breath as Lacy slipped over beside the truck and gently opened the door. The interior light didn't come on. A moment later Lacy was back, grinning. "Yup, keys are in it."

"Will it work? I noticed the interior light didn't come on."

"I took the bulb out of that long ago; Miranda and I were trying to be sneaky when we were pretending to be Lady Blue."

Penny chuckled and kissed her cheek. "Gods, you're a nut, Lacy. Let's go get our people out."

The major was just turning back toward his captives when something moved through the tent at super speed. A fist cracked against his jaw and he fell to the ground, unconscious. Lacy turned from her victim and began to get the restraints off the woman. Penny had already released the man. "All right, folks, let's go."

She led them outside and to Lacy's truck. Lacy handed the man the major's hat and jacket. "Put these on, you're driving."

He nodded, slipped on the disguise and climbed behind the wheel. Lacy got in the back with the woman. Penny was already in the front passenger's seat, a gun in her hand. "If the disguise doesn't work, make a run for it and I'll try to hold them off with this. We really don't want them to know who brought you out."

"Oh, why not?"

"Tell you later, let's go. What's your name?"

"Andy Blaise," he replied as he started the truck.

"Pleased to meet you Andy, I've heard lots of good things about you. I'm Penny and that's Lacy in the back. Nice and easy now."

"Gotcha." He drove slowly to the check point leading to the road to the city. Two armed soldiers blocked his way, but he stopped, opened the door and leaned out, waving them off. "Get the hell out of the way." They stepped back and saluted as the truck rolled by.

As Andy picked up speed and turned onto the road, his three passengers sat back up. "That was great, Andy," grinned Penny.

"Thanks. So, who are you really, super woman?"

"Lady Blue, and that's Lady Warrior in the back."

"So, you're Miranda's mom," said Lacy, smiling brightly at the frightened woman. "Relax now, you're with family, you're safe."

"Family? Are you a friend of Miranda's?"

"Yes, Ma'am, I'm your daughter in law, Lacy Bevan."

"My daughter in law? You're the one Miranda keeps talking about, the Lady Warrior."

"Yep, that's me."

"Is Miranda all right? Is she safe?"

"Yes Ma'am, our girl is quite safe, I promise. She's with Lady Justice in Georgia City, safe behind the shield. So, how did you end up a prisoner here?"

"Jean, call me Jean. It was horrible. Men in police uniforms smashed in our door, shot my husband, then put a bag over my head and dragged me away. I remember being on an airplane, then here in that tent. We've been there for days."

"How about you, Andy?"

"Same story, Lacy," he replied. "I got a call from my ex-wife, said she wanted to meet and talk. She sounded upset, so I went to meet her. Found three guys with guns instead. Is Seeker okay? Did she make it out?"

"Yep, she's in Georgia city with Justice, safe and sound. Okay, Andy, hang a left onto the highway, we'll get you two back to safety behind that shield before we do anything else. You okay with that, Penny?"

"Absolutely. Let's take these folks home then we can drive back in this pretty truck of yours like you wanted to in the first place."

Lacy laughed at that.

"Her truck?" asked Andy.

"I took it off a pair of second rate thieves a couple of years ago," said Lacy. "I've got lots of miles and good memories of this truck, and I was pissed we had to drive around in that old wreck. I was whining to Penny about it when we found the military camp where you were held prisoner. We sneaked in for a look and found you guys. We needed a getaway vehicle and there was my baby, just waiting for us."

Andy chuckled at that. "Seeker always says it's better to be lucky than good."

"Yeah," said Lacy. "I'm surprised Lenni hasn't ..." her phone buzzed in her pocket. "Bet that's her now." She swiped it on. "Lacy."

"Lacy, Lenora tells me you're in the back seat of a truck with another woman. You'd better not be snuggling with Penny or I'll rat you out to Tara."

"No, Miranda honey, no, I'm being good. I'm sitting here chatting with my mother in law."

"What??? Lacy ..."

"Easy sweetheart. Penny and I found a military camp just outside the buffer zone. They were holding your mom and Lenni's friend Andy, hostage. They were hoping for you to make a rescue attempt so they could take you out. Penny and I busted the hostages out and used our truck to make our getaway. We're bringing them home now. Hang on, I'll put her on."

Lacy passed the phone to the woman beside her. "Hello? Miranda?"

"Mom? Is that you? Are you all right?"

"Yes, I'm okay. Your partner rescued us and we're on our way to you. I must say, Miranda, Lacy is quite a woman."

"Yes she is Mom. She's also the world's worst flirt. Lacy, you'd better not be flirting with my mom or you'll be in trouble."

"Lady Watcher, you're a hard woman. I rescued your mom and now you're beating me up."

"I know," replied Miranda, a giggle in her voice. "Whatever are you going to do with me?"

"Oh, I've got a whole list of things to do with you, pretty lady."

"Lacy! For the love of god woman, my mother is right there, behave yourself."

"Yes dear, whatever was I thinking."

"I have no idea, but you can tell me all about it when we get a minute."

"Miranda! For the love of Pete, your mother is right here."

"Lacy?"

"Yeah?"

"You're way too much fun to tease. Listen honey, do you need me and Ellith to come ride shotgun?"

"No, we're clear, sweetie. Andy pretended to be an officer and the guards let us out. We got away clean. Meet us at the shield in about an hour?"

"I'll be there. Here's Seline."

"Lacy, are you certain you're clear?"

"Yes, my goddess, we're clear. We'll drop off our passengers with you then resume our mission."

"All is well then."

The connection broke and Lacy sighed as she dropped the phone back in her pocket.

"Did she really think you and Penny ..."

"No, Jean," chuckled Lacy. "Lenora and I went on a mission together. We were waiting for the enemy to arrive, watching from a hill. It was cold and damp, so I tossed a blanket over Lenni and crawled under with her to stay warm.

"I used to be a professional fighter. I'll fight cold if I have to, but cold muscles can cramp up and get injured. Anyway, that brat Miranda used her magic vision to check on the mission and saw us snuggled up together. She's teased me mercilessly about that ever since. The girl's relentless."

"Lacy, you sound so proud of her."

"I am, Jean. I love the girl to distraction. Miranda's more precious to me than life itself, she makes me crazy in the most delightful way, and she's a terrible tease. It's good I can wear red gracefully."

"I'm so delighted to hear that, for she rarely smiled through most of her young life. I'm glad she has you, Lacy."

"We just crossed the border into the buffer zone, folks," said Penny. "We're about ten minutes from the city and the Shield."

THE REUNION WAS SWEET and still going on when they left for North Bay once again. "We'll be near that military camp in a few minutes," said Penny, gazing out the window. "How do you want to handle it if they try to stop us?"

"They'll get a quick introduction to Lady Warrior if they do."

"Lacy?"

"Sorry, Penny, but like I said, I like this truck. I was thinking of asking Dex to soup it up for me like he did Vic's new viper."

"Come on, Lacy, it's just a truck."

"No it isn't."

Penny turned to give Lacy her full attention. "Hey, talk to me, sister, what's so darn special about this truck?"

"It's where Miranda and I first got together, where we spent our first few months together on the road. Call it a sentimental attachment. I'll bet you've still got that motorcycle you and Tara first rode."

"It's in the garage at Mamma's house in New York," replied Penny, reaching over to pat Lacy's arm. "Okay, sis, we keep the truck no matter what."

"Thanks, Penny. Pissed at me?"

"Nope, not even a little bit. I understand now, and yes, I'd want to keep it too. Oh crap, here they come. Play it cool."

"Okay, but ..."

"Yeah, I know. Pull over now, they're blocking the road."

Four soldiers with weapons pointed at them blocked the road. Lacy coasted to a stop right beside them and rolled down the window. "Hi guys, what's up?"

"Get out of the vehicle, now."

"No, what for? We haven't done anything wrong."

"You're driving a stolen truck, now get out and get on the ground."

"What the hell do you mean, stolen? This is my boyfriend's truck."

"That truck was in a military compound under guard until last night."

"The hell it was. We've been trapped in Georgia City for the past few weeks, goddam shield up and couldn't get out. I don't know what truck you had, buddy, but this ain't it."

The soldier hesitated. She could be telling the truth. "Excuse me, sir," said Penny. "Can you tell me why we would drive right by your camp with a stolen truck we took from you? How do you imagine the two of us managed to get a truck out of your guarded compound anyway?"

"Come on, man," said Lacy. "Think about this." He gazed into her eyes for a long moment then lowered his weapon and motioned for the others to move the jeep. As soon as the way was clear he waved them through.

"Morons," grinned Lacy as they drove away towards North Bay. A half hour later they were in the city. "Let's take a cruise around, see what we can see."

"Works for me."

What they saw sickened them. The attack and ensuing battles had devastated the city. Streets had been torn up, sewage systems badly damaged, and there were burned out vehicles everywhere. The old entrance to the mansion was gone and the property nothing but an empty crater.

Down by the waterfront it was worse. Everything for two whole blocks had been flattened. Stray dogs and feral cats could be seen feeding on rotting corpses. There had been no attempt to clean up the mess, dispose of the bodies, or rebuild anything, it had all been left as it was.

Lacy was muttering under her breath as they drove past the rubble where the mission had stood. Further on, they found looters hard at work. Up into the better parts of town the people looked to be under siege, defending their homes against roving gangs of looters. Finally, Penny sighed and pulled out her phone. She made a full report to Lady Shadow.

"That's the size of it, Seline. I'd say this town needs a big dose of the Viper plus Decoy and his troops. What do you want us to do?"

"I'll send Viper and the troops through to you, Penny. I want you to re-take the city for me. Keep Lacy there, Miranda will remain here for the moment."

"Hey now ..."

"Miranda, I must keep you safe, you're the dark's primary target."

"All right, but as soon as Decoy gets that second shield in place I want to be back in North Bay."

Lady Shadow chuckled. "I guess that's a fair compromise, my fierce sister. Did you hear all that, Penny?"

"Got it, Boss. Get the shield up then let Miranda take the city."

"Prepare, they will begin arriving immediately." As soon as Lady Shadow finished speaking a bright light appeared and a jet black viper roared through.

Taking the City

The big car came to a stop right beside Penny. "What's the drill, Lady Blue?"

"The city has gone to hell, Vic. The police were devastated in the Fishman war and I'm sure they lost more men in this last attack. Once the military pulled out chaos ensued, gangs appearing everywhere, looters, ... you get the idea.

"Just drive around a bit, let them see you, bully a few gangs, you know, do Viper stuff."

"Viper stuff coming right up," he grinned. His armor popped up and the engine revved, then the tires squealed in protest as he raced away.

As Viper drove away the soldiers began to appear from the portal. The last two were carrying the shield generator. Lady Shadow followed then the portal vanished. "Decoy, put the generator in Lacy's truck, find a likely spot and get it set up."

"Yes, Ma'am. I know just the spot. The place where your headquarters used to be is central to the city. That would be the best placement for the shield."

"You'll need materials and supplies to make that place secure. Penny, contact Ryder and ask her to send Dex through. He should be able to supply whatever Decoy needs."

"On it, Boss. Where will you be?"

"Hunting," she replied then vanished.

"I sure don't envy whoever she's hunting for," sighed Decoy. "Okay, Lacy, we're loaded up. Let's go. Sergeant Perkins, secure this area and hold until I return."

The man saluted then started bawling orders. The soldiers were soon inside a building, out of sight of passersby. Decoy jumped into the back of the truck with the shield generator and the three soldiers there.

"Damn, they sure made a mess of this place," muttered Decoy as he gazed at the devastation where the gates once stood. He walked up to the lip of the crater where the original mansion had stood before Shadow moved it off world. "What'd you think, Lacy? Right here?"

"I like it, Decoy. It's on a hill so it'll get lots of sunlight for power, and the big foxhole should be easy enough to defend."

"Big foxhole," he grinned. "Yeah, I like it. Bring it up, guys."

The two men carried the generator into the crater, settled it onto a stable position, then one set the dials and turned it on. "Okay, she's on, now to find out for sure it's working."

"We'll do it, Decoy," said Penny. "We'll check it out then call you before we head to the police station."

They trotted down the hill and jumped in the truck. A few minutes' drive put them at the edge of town where a police car was parked with lights flashing. Several cars were in various stages of damage, the shield was working. Grinning, Penny pulled out her phone while Lacy turned the truck around.

They popped up the armor as they arrived at the police station, then walked inside to face sudden drawn guns and aggressive shouting police officers. When the two armored women didn't obey instructions, guns were fired, tazers as well, all to no effect. "Waste of time," said Lacy. "As y'all can see, the armor's bullet proof."

At that point a big man tackled her, but Lacy easily tossed him aside. "That's enough," said Penny. "I'm Lady Blue, and this is Lady Warrior. Stand down now or get hurt."

"Stand down," shouted the police chief as he appeared from his office. "Stand down. All right, Lady Blue, what do you want?"

"Relax, Chief, I bring you good news. This city is now under a shield like the one at Georgia City. Warrior and I have come at the request of Lady Shadow to take control of the city. Your force is struggling to regain control, we're here to help you.

"The soldiers of Justice have also returned and will work with you to maintain control. Their commander is a man named Decoy. He'll contact you shortly. Also, the Viper has returned, he'll put a stop to the gangs and the looting."

"Yes, and kill hundreds while he's at it."

"Maybe yes, maybe no," said Lacy. "You see, Viper hates gangs, and he has his reasons. If these people behave, they've got nothing to fear from Viper. We brought him back because by his very presence he will greatly reduce the incidents of gang violence and robbery."

The chief sighed and leaned against the counter. "I guess it doesn't matter anymore, does it. The MPs said we're a separate country now, owned by Lady Shadow. The laws we tried to uphold mean nothing now. I guess we just wait until Shadow brings down the new rules."

"For now the old rules continue to apply, with a few notable exceptions. Viper is out of bounds, and so are the Soldiers of Justice. In truth, if I were you I'd be expecting a visit from Lady Justice in the near future," said Penny.

The chief swallowed hard and several officers took a step back from them. "Lady Justice?"

"Yeah, I think Lady Shadow will probably hand over the running of both cities to Tasha. They think alike, you see. Neither one of them has any time for a lot of BS, and they both believe in justice, cold hard justice.

"So, with that in mind, here's the deal Justice offered the police in Georgia City. It'll work the same way here. If you can't live with her style of handling police brutality, or her way of enforcing the law, take off the uniform and head to the edge of the shield. Arrangements will be made to let you leave the city.

"However, if you feel you'd make a good peace keeper, stick around, it should prove interesting. Now, we'll leave you folks to spread the word and mull over the decision. Remember, the commander of the Soldiers is a man named Decoy. He'll contact you soon.

"Okay, it's been fun, but we've got stuff to do. You might want to reinforce the poor guys out at the edge of the shield. It's getting busy out there." As she finished speaking Penny and Lacy blurred out of sight leaving the police to mull over what had just happened.

Back by the shield generator things were getting busy. Ryder had brought a few of the Chosen along with Dex to see if they could help out. There was a large portal shining as Lacy pulled up. Soldiers and the Chosen were carrying bundles of materials into the open area of the crater, as well as the surrounding trees.

"Hey there, where's Miranda?" asked Penny.

"Out on dragon back, helping Viper to get things under control," replied one of the soldiers.

"So, what's all this?" asked Lacy.

"Dex is outfitting us," grinned Decoy. "I've got no idea at all what this stuff is. But he says we need it. I trust the guy, so ..."

The arrival of two speeders interrupted him. "Hi guys," called Ryder as she hopped off her speeder. "Man, that Viper sure puts the fear into the bad guys. You should see it. People cowering while the looters steal everything in sight, then Vic rides up and jumps out of the car, a gun in each hand. He doesn't say anything, doesn't do anything, just stands there.

"Everybody stops what they're doing. He points at the building and the looters start putting stuff back. When they finish they run away. Vic gets back in the car and goes to another hot spot, same thing. Shit, he even scares me when he does that silent avenger thing."

They laughed with her then Dex returned with the last of the supplies. With the aid of three enhanced warriors the camp and defenses were soon set up and ready.

IT TOOK LONGER THAN expected for Lady Shadow to find what she sought, a faint trail of her own energy. Eyes closed tightly, she focused on following that thin ribbon of energy. In time she arrived on a stark and lonely cliff overlooking a wild churning ocean below. This was Earth, but not Earth as anyone would know it. It was another Earth in another universe, and a different timeline, a young Earth, a raw Earth.

Opening her eyes, she found what she sought, the mansion she and her people called home. Seline'd had no real idea where it had gone, she'd just flung it out into the unknown to protect it from being destroyed. It sat there, precariously perched on the edge of the cliff, cold, eerie, empty of life.

Tossing her thick braid back from her shoulder, Shadow walked to the door and stepped inside. All was as they had left it that fateful morning, coffee cups still partly full of cold dark liquid, breakfast half eaten, pieces of clothing tossed aside in haste and more. Showing no emotion at all she moved through the rooms.

Shadow stopped halfway up the stairs to Miranda's tower, exactly in the spot where Moragah had warned her and forced her to reach for more power than she'd ever wanted. She was now a goddess, albeit a reluctant goddess. Gently her hand caressed the wall where she'd leaned as she released her grip on mortality and accepted her fate.

She paused there, allowing it all to sink in deeper, fighting back the tide of emotion and fear that threatened to overwhelm her. A goddess, all powerful, immortal, and because of that she would live to see all she knew, the people she loved, fade into time and pass away. She had sacrificed everything she was to grant those she cherished a few more years of existence.

With heavy steps she resumed the climb to the tower, it was still there, although the link to the mansion was greatly weakened. She closed her eyes and renewed that link until it was shining brightly once again, then she sat in Miranda's chair and morphed back into Seline Elmore.

"Come on girl, get a grip on yourself. You can't let it beat you down, not now. Right now they still exist, they're still in danger, and they need you. Pull yourself together and get back in the game. There'll be time enough to mourn them a few hundred years from now."

With a deep sigh of resignation, she arose and became the goddess Shadow once again. She spread her arms wide and began drawing deep breaths, focusing her mind, her power, the sheer force of her will.

In a wide spot near where Decoy was overseeing the set up of his encampment, a blinding light appeared. When the light faded there stood the mansion, just as it had before. Lady Shadow appeared beside it, mounted on the dragon's back.

The mighty beast roared and spat flame, the scrub trees and bushes between the mansion and the road melted away, and a rough driveway was left behind. Shadow smiled with delight as the wild cheering from Ryder, Penny, and Lacy lifted the darkness from her heart. She was home again.

THE CHIEF OF POLICE sat in his office, brooding. How had this all happened? American forces attacking an American city? What the hell had prompted that? They'd put out some cock and bull story about a deadly virus to the rest of the country, but that was pure bullshit. They'd been after Lady Shadow.

For Christ's sake, it had been Shadow and her allies that has saved the city from the invasion of the fishmen. His own forces had been decimated by the South American gang that came as part of that invasion. They'd still been rebuilding the force when the military attack came. Now he faced an even more uncertain future.

The chief's reverie was broken by a soft knock on his door. "Come."

"Sir, that private detective is here to see you, Seline Elmore."

The chief sighed and turned back to the room as he rose from his chair. "Send her in."

Smiling brightly, she entered and took the chair he indicated. "So, Miss Elmore, what brings you out of hiding?"

"A world gone utterly crazy, chief. Have you any idea at all what the hell this is all about?"

"Yes and no. I suspect somebody with a load of clout is after your hide."

"My hide?"

"Your hide, Lady Shadow. You can drop the act with me, I know who you are."

He was stunned at what happened next, she dropped the act, stood and morphed into the shadow warrior. "Very well then, so be it. There will be no further charades between us. Now, Lady Justice has already dealt with the rogue general who ordered the attacks on Georgia City and North Bay, however, the man who controlled him has vanished.

"At the battle of the fishmen we managed to capture the man behind the invasion, one Mr. Kaufman. I dealt with him myself. This latest attack was orchestrated by his brother, but this Mr. Kaufman has eluded me. Have you any idea at all where he may be found?"

The chief sighed and leaned back in his chair. "None."

"What do you know of the Brotherhood?"

"I have no idea what you're talking about."

She glanced beside him and he looked where she was focused. He swallowed hard and froze in place, there was a huge cobra right behind his chair. The snake didn't move and she nodded, waved her hand, and it crawled into the shadows then disappeared.

"That was Minx," she said in answer to his unasked question. "Had you lied to me he would have struck. Very well, I believe I can trust you. As you are aware, we have re-taken the city. I want you to continue to rebuild your force and to keep the peace here.

"My soldiers will assist you until you have the police back at full strength. Viper will keep the scum in line and I'll ask Lady Blue to organize and rule the city. You will report to her directly. Will you do this for me?"

"Sure, why the hell not? You've done more to protect this city than the government has. Can you tell me what you really are, where you came from?"

"I am Lady Shadow, and I come from the imagination of a goddess. My apologies if that doesn't really help."

She had a slight grin on her face and he chuckled. "I suppose that's as good an answer as I'll ever get. Can you tell me what the Brotherhood is?"

"It is a secret society dedicated to total world domination. It is ancient and has many arms. I believe the Kaufman brothers to be mere pawns of the Brotherhood, as was the general.

"I'm here in this world as an agent of balance, trying to push back the darkness until the forces of light and dark are on a more equal footing. The Brotherhood is a tool of the darkness, and thus means to stop me. I, on the other hand, intend to make an end of them."

"So, the Brotherhood is the bad guy, and you're the good."

"Simply put, but inherently accurate, yes. So, we are in agreement? You'll work with us?"

"As I said, you and your people have done more for this city in the past few years than the government has ever done. I'm your man."

"Excellent, Decoy will set up a meeting with Lady Blue for you." With that she morphed back into Seline Elmore and walked to the door. "Thanks again for seeing me, Chief." With that she was gone.

The police lieutenant had seen her leave. He stepped into the chief's office. "Chief, did I just see that PI, Seline Elmore, leaving your office?"

"You did."

"What did she want?"

"She wanted to know when it would be possible to leave the city. I told her I had no idea, then she probed me for information. She's on the trail of some billionaire. Now how the hell would I know where a billionaire would hide?"

"So, we get anything new from those soldiers?"

"Nothing yet. That commander told me to sit tight, we should be able to get access and egress through the shield by tomorrow. He also said to stay away from Viper, he's cleaning out the gangs and looters. Must be true cause we haven't had a call in hours."

"The fucking Viper. Who knew that killer would turn out to be a more effective police officer that any of us. The whole world's gone to hell."

"Can't argue that," said his lieutenant as he stepped out and closed the office door.

"ME? YOU WANT ME TO be queen of the city?"

"Come on, Penny, you know you want to," grinned Seline. "I need Miranda back in her tower, and I need Ellen working with me ..."

Penny was laughing now. "All right, sister, I'll do it, but I warn you, I just might enjoy the job."

Tracking the Enemy

B y nightfall Lady Shadow had brought all her people back to the mansion. She'd left Tasha with her people intact and had sent the Chosen to Georgia City to help as well since she was pulling so many out to North Bay. Once again the living room of the mansion looked like a family conference.

Debbie smiled as she set out coffee for everybody. "Seline, I have to tell you, I didn't think we'd ever get this back. It's good to be home again." The others all agreed. "Can I ask you a dumb question?"

"Sure. Shoot."

"How did you get the power, sewer, and water hooked up so quickly?"

Seline laughed with delight. "Okay, it's a bit of a cheat. The power is a power pack from Eelion, so is the sewage treatment. The water is a direct hook into a river in another dimension. This way, even if they cut everything off, it won't affect us."

"So, let's share. Vic, report."

"Okay, well, things were pretty quiet in Georgia City when I left, with me cruising daytimes, Tasha roaming at night, and the Chosen all over the place, the baddies were laying pretty low. Same here. They see that viper on the street and they melt away, plus they're learning fast the Chosen mean business."

"Miranda?"

"I'm just so thrilled the tower survived. I've been looking everywhere, and that military camp just outside the city seems to be the only dark spot left. One dark one in particular, probably the man in command. As far as the tower goes, everything survived intact."

"Ellen?"

"We beat them, honey, we beat them and all of us survived. Sadly, a lot of innocent people didn't. The city is in rough shape, but we've regained control. You've forced them to back off, so personally, I'd say we've got a breather, time to up our defenses, see if we can root out some of the brotherhood."

"Penny?"

"Yeah, well, I was doing good as Lady Blue, slipping around the mean streets, beating up bad guys after dark, stuff like that, then I signed on with Lady Shadow. She made me mayor and now I'm up to my ass in bureaucracy. How do I get a transfer out of here?"

Everybody was having a good laugh at that. "Aw come on, Penny," grinned Seline, "admit it, you're having fun. No more hiding in alleys, sleeping behind dumpsters, now you have a big office, get to sleep in a bed, ..."

"Thanks be for that," said Tara Montrose, Penny's partner.

"Okay, yeah, I'm good with it," smiled Penny, "there's some highly skilled people to take care of the small stuff. I can deal. So, what happened with Jack Longtree?"

"He signed on with the Chosen," said Ryder. "It seemed like a good fit. At first he wanted to go home, but he'd be too easy a target there, so I offered him colors. He's earned them."

"Yes he has," agreed Lenora. "Okay, my turn. Seline, my sister, you've put Mary-jo and Uncle Morty in the guest rooms. Is there anything we can do for them?"

"As I understand it, they lost everything just as you got them out, is that right?"

"Yeah, it is. We have nothing to go back to, none of us. I get the sense you want me here anyway, am I right?"

Seline morphed back into Lady Shadow. "Yes, my sister, I do need you here. You and I will hunt together now. Lacy, I will want you at my side as well. Ryder, I know you want to go back west, but ..."

"You want the Chosen in Georgia City?"

"Yes, for the time being, I do."

"Then that's where we'll stay, Lady Shadow."

"Excellent, Ryder. Thank you. Now, Heather, ask your friends to remain as our guests for a few days more then we'll turn our attention to their needs. Lenora, I need you to find a man for me."

"Show me the bugger, I'll find him." Lady Shadow waved her arm and a hologram of a man appeared. "That's Mr. Kaufman, Shadow, you took him away yourself, you know where he is."

"Yes, it's his brother I want now. Can you get a fix on him from this?"

"Should be able to. Give me a minute." Lenora began to slowly turn in a circle, all the time talking to the man. "Mr. Kaufman, where are you, you murderous bastard, talk to me. Where are you? Crap, I'm not getting anything. Come on, Kaufman, talk to me, you miserable fucker."

She stopped moving, backed up a bit, then forward. "Gotcha. Far away, so far away, in a safe room, no, a cell below a castle, pulling back, yes, the south of Germany." Lenora stopped speaking and began to melt to the floor. Heather caught her and held her up. "Man, that took the good out of me. Just give me a minute, I'll be okay."

"Sit here," said Heather, "I'll get you some water." She hurried away to the kitchen.

Lady Shadow reached out to lay her hand on Lenora's shoulder. Suddenly a wave of loving healing energy flowed into Lenora, almost as though Moragah had done it. Wide eyed she gazed up at Shadow. Heather reappeared with the water and Lenora thanked her then drank it.

"Lenora, is our friend in Germany heavily guarded?"

"Yes. I believe he's a prisoner. I'm thinking the Brotherhood doesn't like failure."

"I agree with your assessment. Penny, will you need Lacy here with you for a short while?"

"No, I've got Miranda and Vic to help keep a lid on things."

"Excellent. I'll have Lenora and Lacy back to you as soon as we have our quarry. Come, my sisters, we're going sightseeing." Lenora and Lacy stepped close and then all three vanished.

THEY REAPPEARED IN a forested hillside. "This place is in Germany, my sisters. Lenora, tune in on our quarry now, see if you can find him."

It took her mere moments. "Yes, there he is. He's still a good way off, but I can find him easily now."

"Then perhaps we will ride the rest of the way on dragon back. Aeroth." The huge beast coalesced from the shadows. Shadow leaped to her place on his back then pulled the other two up behind. "Think of the place now, Lady Seeker. See it in your mind. Aeroth, have you got the location?"

For an answer the dragon screamed a challenge and leaped into the air. A few beats of mighty wings and then the ground below seemed to shift, they were looking down at a well-guarded castle.

Gunfire erupted from below as the dragon settled slowly to the ground within the keep. The three armored warriors leaped from its back and went on the offensive. The guards in the immediate area were soon thinned out and the guns fell silent. "Lenora, where?"

"This way." Before she could take a step, the Warrior sped past her. More gunfire was heard then silence.

"Lenora, you and Lacy find and secure our quarry, I have another errand. I'll return to you as quickly as possible." With that, Lady Shadow vanished.

Lacy came down off combat mode, her armor spattered with gore. "Which way?"

"There." Lenora pointed the way and the Warrior cleared away the opposition. Several turns, three sets of stairs, and five barred doors later, they found the locked cells. Lacy was still spoiling for a fight, but there was no one left to oppose her. They located Mr. Kaufman's cell and Lenora ripped the door off it then stepped inside.

"Mr. Kaufman, I presume," grinned Lacy as she grabbed the cringing man by the collar.

"Bring him, Lacy. We'll take him up topside where the dragon can land."

"Dragon?" whimpered the hapless man.

"Yeah," chuckled Lacy. "You'll have to watch out for him, he drools."

THE SOUND OF GUNFIRE sent the scarlet robed figures scurrying towards the exits, but the doors to the room were locked. They couldn't get out. Panic continued to rise as they grabbed chairs and attacked the doors, all to no avail. Eventually, the grandmaster regained order, pounding on his table with a gavel and shouting. Slowly, the men returned to their places at the table.

As they resumed their seats, one man gasped and pointed at the shadows in the corner. A figure was coalescing there. Several guns appeared and were emptied into the slowly growing figure, but it ignored them. The figure became a tall female with up swept ears and a thick braid of red hair tossed carelessly over one shoulder. She was wearing gore bespattered metal armor and carrying a staff. "Shadow," said a soft frightened voice.

"Correct, I am Shadow. This is a meeting of the Brotherhood, yes?"

No one answered. "I am aware you have my enemy, Mr. Kaufman, confined in the cells below. I also assume that, since you took him prisoner, you are his superiors in that accursed organization. You there, are you indeed the head of the Brotherhood?" Still no one spoke.

"Very well, perhaps I should be more persuasive." She tossed her staff onto the table where it instantly became a huge cobra. The snake rose up and flared its hood. "This is Minx. He will bite anyone who lies to me, and his bite is fatal."

Everyone was cringing away from her now. "I should also point out that a refusal to respond will be viewed by the snake as a lie of omission." She gave them a minute to let that sink in then she spoke again. "I ask again, sir, are you indeed the head of the Brotherhood?"

"No," he stammered. The snake didn't move.

"I see. Are you the most senior member of the Brotherhood in this room?"

"Yes."

"Is there a more highly placed man in the immediate area of this castle or nearby town?"

"No."

Slowly she nodded her head. "Is everyone in this room a member of the Brotherhood?"

"Yes."

"What is the name of your superior and where do I find him?"

"I don't know." The snake struck, fastening its fangs deeply into the man's neck. He screamed and fought, but to no avail. He soon lay still and the snake returned to the table.

"Does anyone here know the name and/or the location of this man's superior?"

They all denied it and the snake didn't move. "Very well then," she said as she swept the snake into her hand where it became a staff again, "we're finished here. Aeroth!" At her call the dragon moved from the shadows, sending the men scurrying for the doors once again.

"Aeroth, cleanse this place." At her command the beast screamed a challenge then spat hellfire into the room. She waved her arm and both she and the dragon reappeared outside in the courtyard. The entire castle was now in flames.

Lady Shadow looked around and saw Lenora leading Lacy and her prisoner out of the burning building. Shadow created a shining portal. "Aeroth, take Lacy and Seeker back to the mansion. I'll be along shortly." She grabbed Mr. Kaufman by the collar and they both disappeared. The two warriors climbed to the dragon's back and he leaped into the air then flew through the portal.

They reappeared at the front door of the mansion. As they slid to the ground Lacy felt something wet drop onto her shirt. She turned to face the dragon, it almost looked like it was laughing. "Did you just drool on me? My god, you did, you drooled on me."

Lenora was laughing, and the dragon's great body shook as though he was too. Suddenly Aeroth's tongue flicked out and, ever so lightly, caressed Lacy's cheek. Lacy laughed with them and patted him on the neck. "You're just lucky you're cute, buddy." He gave her a gentle nudge then disappeared into the shadows.

LADY SHADOW AND HER captive reappeared on an alien planet. There had once been a thriving civilization here, but now all lay in ruins, destroyed. A few creatures could be seen staggering about, searching through the rubble, wailing with heart reading sorrow as they found the remains of loved ones lost.

"Where are we?"

"On another planet far from Earth."

"Why have you brought me here?"

"I have questions, and I believe you may have the answers."

"I won't tell you anything, I'll die first."

"You suddenly seem almost anxious to embrace death, why the hurry?"

He sighed and sank to the ground, shaking. "It's all gone, everything, all the money, wealth, and power stripped away by the Brotherhood, because of you. You killed my brother, and now you've destroyed me. Just kill me and get it over with."

"You blame me for your misfortune, and yet it was you who attacked me and my people. Why?"

"Why? Why wouldn't we? You were hunting us, killing us off one by one. You killed my brother. Why wouldn't I want revenge."

"It may surprise you to know your brother is probably still alive."

"What? Alive? Where?"

"His greatest wish was to be the most wealthy and powerful man in the world, so I put him on an empty world, much like this one will become in a few centuries. There was plenty of food and water there, so he could easily survive, and as the only man alive on that world, his wish was granted. Do you wish to be united with him?"

"Yes, oh god, yes. Look, I'll make a deal with you. Reunite me with my brother, put us back on Earth, in America, and I'll tell you everything I know."

"Look beside you, on the ground. See that small snake?"

"Yes," he replied, easing away from the creature.

"Its bite is fatal. If you lie to me or bargain in bad faith, he will strike. I ask you now, was that offer genuine?"

"Yes."

Shadow looked to the tiny snake, but it hadn't moved. "If I do as you ask, how do you hope to escape the Brotherhood?"

"I don't know, but I do have a few allies, friends. At least there we'll have a fighting chance. With luck you will keep their attention elsewhere."

"Very well then, I accept your offer." Her armor disappeared, and she was dressed in flowing robes of forest green. "Touch my robe." He tentatively reached out to grasp the sleeve of her robe and they both vanished.

They reappeared on a different planet. There wasn't much to see except the remains of an ancient civilization, grown over and most absorbed by time. "Look there, your brother survives."

Kaufman looked where she pointed and saw a figure, foraging from the vegetation growing over the ruins. Running toward the man, he called out his name. The man turned and stumbled away in fear. "It may take you some time to gain his trust. I'll leave you here for now, and then return to finish fulfilling our bargain." With that, she vanished.

Suddenly lost and terrified at the woman's disappearance, he stood gazing at the place where she'd stood. A familiar voice sounded behind him. "Who are you? I can help you find food." He turned to face the half-starved visage of his once all-powerful brother. "David? Is that you? Did she catch you too?"

He grabbed the gaunt apparition and hugged him closely. "Yes, Stanton, it is I. The Brotherhood took me prisoner because I failed to kill her. She rescued me and brought me here."

"David? Why did you attack her? After what happened to me, why ...?

"I had no choice. The Brotherhood sent me a clear message, kill her or be killed. I failed. I was still mourning you, my brother, and I was vengeful. I used Slevin to attack both their strongholds, even went after the outriders, the bounty hunter and the motorcycle gang. He failed, and I was blamed."

"But you're alive, and here now. It takes time to get used to being alone but won't be so bad for you. I'm here with you."

"We won't be alone for long, Stanton. I've struck a bargain with her. I'll spill my guts to her about the Brotherhood, and she'll take us back to Earth."

"That was foolish, David." He allowed his thin shoulders to sag. "You can't trust her."

"What's the alternative, Stanton? Remain here and wait for her patience to run out then face torture or worse at her hands? No, we take our chances."

"At least insist that she return us before you sign our death warrants. The Brotherhood will know. They'll hunt us then execute us."

"Not if she stops them first. Think, Stanton, she's beaten them at every turn. I was held in Germany, but she tracked me there and destroyed Eiger and the rest of the European elite. She can do it, brother. She can bring the once mighty Brotherhood to its knees. We will survive this, we'll be back at the reins of power before you know it, only this time we won't have to dance the Brotherhood's tune. We'll be the ones in control. We will."

His brother didn't look convinced, but he would have many days to convince him while they waited for Lady Shadow to return.

THE FOLK WERE GATHERED in the living room when Shadow returned and morphed back into Seline. "Hey kids, any of that coffee for me?"

"Right here, lover," smiled Ellen as she patted the couch beside her and pulled a full mug close for Seline.

Sinking into the sofa beside Ellen, Seline took a long sip from the mug and sighed with contentment. "Lenora and Lacy get back okay?"

"Yes, they're in the kitchen having a snack," said Heather. "I'll go rescue some for you."

"Cool. I'll save my report until they can join us. Anything interesting happen while I was gone?"

"Well," smiled Ellen, "Vic got into it with a street gang, they're a number of members short right now. I think they got the message. Decoy and the Chief of Police met with Penny, that went well, and Miranda went after that Major out at the military camp."

"She did what? Is she ..."

"She's fine, relax now. He's now in Georgia City awaiting Tasha's pleasure. Miranda got back a few minutes ago."

"Oooh, that girl. I told her to be careful; we need her in that tower."

"Relax, I checked everything before I left," sang Miranda as she entered the room. "Besides, you took Lacy and Lenni with you, so I was all alone with no girl to snuggle with."

Seline chuckled. "All right, my fierce sister. Confess now, what did you do?"

"Well, I heard that the military were selling off everything they'd looted from the city. I put on something sexy, then headed out that way and joined the crowd of buyers. It was like a well-guarded flea market. I poked around for a while until I spotted the major giving me the eye.

"I showed him a little cleavage, flirted shamelessly until he invited me back to his tent. Once inside I popped up my armor, decked him, and took him to Tasha through one of the portals. Then I cam home. See, easy money, no problem."

"You took a heck of a risk, sister. What if he'd recognized you?"

"Recognized me? How the hell could he recognize me? He never once looked above my chest. I'll bet he couldn't recognize me even now."

"If he's even alive."

"Yeah, well, he's the bastard who took my mom prisoner. I'm hoping Tasha got some useful information from him then dealt out the justice as only she can do it."

"I can't argue that," replied Seline as Lenora and Lacy returned to the gathering. "Hi guys, you get back all right? You have time for a cuddle before Miranda got home?"

"Naw, she was already here when we got home," replied Lenora then she shrieked as Miranda threw a cushion at her. "Actually, we had no trouble at all, except for when Aeroth drooled on Lacy."

"He what?"

"I made some crack about the dragon drool when we took Kaufman out of his cell. Aeroth must have heard me. How was I supposed to know dragons have super hearing? Anyway, the big guy brought us home in style, no problems. You get anything out of Kaufman?"

"Mr. Kaufman and I have made an agreement. I've already united him with his brother, and next I'll return them to Earth. In exchange, he'll tell me all he knows of the Brotherhood, and name as many members as he can.

"While you guys were bringing Kaufman out, I questioned and eliminated the gathering of Brotherhood elite in the upper rooms of the castle. They attacked us here, and now we've carried the battle to them. I doubt they'll be so quick to attack us again."

Ellen took Seline's hand in hers. "Honey, do you think it's wise to let the Kaufman brothers go?"

"Who said anything about letting them go? I agreed to reunite them, which I did. I also agreed to return them to Earth, which I will. I didn't say anything about where on Earth I'd bring them."

Ellen grinned with delight. "So, you're going to bring them here?"

"Headquarters of Georgia City will be my first choice. Once I have the information, Tasha can have them. She wants, needs, justice for the innocent who died in those attacks, and she shall have it."

A New Connection

The sun was shining through the windows as Tasha opened her eyes. With a groan she pulled the covers over her head. "Come on, Ms. Mayor," giggled Kara as she pulled the covers away from Tasha. "You've been living in the sewers too long, you need to get some sun. Rise and shine, lover of mine, we can say the morning prayer together."

"Hey," Tasha groaned in protest. "I'm supposed to be the one in charge, so why do you get to beat me up?"

"I'm your wife, it's my job."

That made Tasha laugh. "You're a nut, Kara. Have I mentioned that before?"

"First time today, sweetie. Come on, up and at 'em. Day's a wasting." Tasha rose gracefully from the bed and joined Kara at the window. They raised their arms and chanted the morning prayer to Moragah in perfect unison. Still, she didn't answer, and sadly, they turned away.

"I know I shouldn't, but I always feel a bit let down when she doesn't respond," sighed Kara.

"Yeah, me too. Honey, do you think we should say a prayer to Shadow?"

"She said not to, but, sometimes I kind of want to."

"Want to try?"

"Sure, why not. What's the worst that could happen? Let's do it, but not at the window in the sun. Drop the shades, we'll do it in the shadows." Tasha stepped to the window and lowered the shade.

Kara took a deep breath then raised her arms. "Great Lady Shadow, Goddess of Balance and Protector of the People, we, your sisters greet you this morning. We thank you for your protection and guidance. May you name be revered this day."

To their great surprise they heard her soft voice. "My beloved sisters, thank you for that blessing. I will hold you both in my heart this day. I promise that one day soon I'll do my utmost to return Moragah to us. Until then, know that I am with you always."

"Holy crap," breathed Tasha.

"You can say that again."

"Holy crap. Kara, did big sis just reveal something to us?"

"Ah-huh, she sure did. Honey, we've always suspected Seline was way more than she let anybody know. When the military attacked I felt a change in her."

"Yeah, me too, like she'd gotten really pissed and let go of whatever was holding her back."

"Ah-huh, that would be it. She truly is a goddess, and now I think she's beginning to accept that. I'm also thinking Moragah saw this coming and provided us with a warrior goddess to make sure we all survived."

"I have no idea what all is going on, the big picture, but I just got a big dose of reassurance. I've always known that, if it all went down ugly, Moragah wouldn't be able to stop it, to help me."

"And now?"

"Kara, you and I both know Shadow would walk through hell to save any one of us. For me, the big bad world just got a little more secure."

"Yeah, it did. Okay, we have to shake this off. We've got a city to run."

"Right, the city. Okay, but you have to feed me first, then you can drag my sorry butt to city hall and make me face the hordes."

PENNY AND TARA HAD arisen and raised their arms to recite the morning prayer to Moragah. "Still no response?" asked Tara as Penny turned away from the window, her shoulders slumping.

"No, nothing," she sighed. "There's a part of me that feels so empty. I can't even begin to express ..."

She stopped speaking as she suddenly heard a soft voice in her mind and felt a strong presence. "I know I'm a poor substitute, and I swear I'll bring Moragah back to us, but for now, just know I'm with you, my sister."

Penny's face lit up with sudden delight, startling Tara. "What is it, Penny?"

"We have a new prayer, Tara. She put her fist against her left shoulder. "For freedom, and for Shadow. May this day bring power and strength to she who walks in shadow, and may her name be blessed."

"Thank you, my sister," came that soft voice, followed by a wave of warm loving energy.

"Seline, you're not a poor substitute, you're the goddess we serve, never doubt that."

"Penny?"

"It was her, Tara. No, Moragah didn't respond to our prayer, but Lady Shadow did."

"Holy crap, she can do that? So, Shadow is getting stronger?"

"Yeah, I think she's starting to stretch herself."

"Then I'm glad she's on our side."

"I sure wish I knew what's going on with Moragah, though."

"As do I, Penny," came Shadow's voice. "I mean to find out this day. Wish me luck."

IT WAS THE SAME FOR the rest of the Sisters of Shadow. Each said her morning prayer to Moragah and received no answer, yet each in turn, for some reason, said a prayer to Lady Shadow, and She responded to each one, sending them loving energy and strengthening the connection between them.

"What is it, sweetheart?" asked Ellen.

Seline sighed and melted into her arms. "They all did it, Ellen. Even though I told them not to, they did it."

"Did what, honey?"

"Prayed to me. It wasn't so much a prayer as a thank you and a blessing. They feel abandoned by Moragah, and they take comfort that I stayed with them."

"So, what did you do?"

"I answered every prayer, strengthened the link to each of them so they can feel it all the time, then I sent them loving energy. They're precious to me, Ellen. All of them. What am I becoming?"

"Yourself, my love. You're becoming your true self, a goddess."

"I never wanted this, I didn't. I just wanted to serve Moragah and ..." she stopped speaking and sat up. "I'm starting to smell a rat, a big loving non-corporeal rat."

"Seline?"

"Moragah. she knew I'd never go all out as long as she was in the picture. She knew I always held back, so she let this go as far as she dared before warning me. For whatever reason, Moragah needs me at full power, the problem here is, I don't think even she understands what that could mean."

"Maybe she does."

"Ellen?"

"Honey, it was Penny who woke Moragah, right? Somewhere far in the past, the darkness beat her, destroyed her priestesses, her people, and put her in a self-induced coma. Maybe she saw that happening again. What if this time she saw it starting to happen, and she created someone who could do what she couldn't."

"Defeat the dark?"

"No, honey, protect her daughters, her priestesses. Think now, after Mai was killed and Tasha nearly finished, Moragah made you, gave you a lot more power than anybody else, a lot more. I doubt she even understands the true reach of your abilities.

"Honey, both the light and the dark hold back on the people they work through because they fear them getting out of control. Moragah gave it all to you and trusted you to remain true. She made you greater than any of them.

"After that she changed the type of priestess she created. She was making the warriors you would need to help you. Think about it, a seeker who can find anybody anywhere, any time? A warrior? A visionary?

"However, I do agree, she probably let this get out of hand to force you to become all you can be."

"Yeah, well she and I need to have a talk." With that she vanished from the bedroom. Smiling, Ellen rose and said her morning prayer to Moragah, and then another to Lady Shadow. The second one earned her a wave of loving energy and a gentle "behave."

ONCE AGAIN LADY SHADOW appeared in the empty cavern. "Moragah, we need to talk."

A wave of loving healing energy swept over her as that vast presence enfolded her, filling her with feelings of joy, being loved, safe, and well supported. "I am here, my child. Do I detect a note of censure in your voice?"

The mother goddess's amusement was easy to read, and Shadow sighed. "So, I amuse your ass, do I?"

"You might, if I actually had such an anatomy. However, I can see that Ellen's insights are as amazing as ever, and you're beginning to understand what was done and why. Seline, there's more to this yet, my sister. More for you to learn."

"All right, so how about you let me in on some of … wait a minute, you called me sister. You've never done that before. Moragah, what are you trying to tell me?"

"You already know, dear Shadow. Allow yourself to embrace the knowledge, the rightness of it, the necessity of it."

"Moragah, I'm beginning to see what I'm capable of, and it frightens me. You, and your compatriots of the light and the dark, are confined here to this world, but I'm not. I can go anywhere, any when, but you're not able to do that. Why did you give me this ability?"

"I didn't, Sister Shadow, you did that on your own. I merely gave you access to your own imagination, the rest you have done on your own. You are free of the bonds that hold us, and you can take the others with you if you need to."

Suddenly a harsh voice interfered. "That all sounds so very sweet, but too bad she is corporeal, she dies here." There was a loud explosion and the entrance to the cavern collapsed. "I've beaten you at last, you stupid abomination. You will perish slowly in this place and I will make sure you do not escape."

"You'd be the voice of the dark, right?" said Seline as Shadow morphed back into her human form.

"I am that, hear me and fear, your fate is sealed."

"Sounds impressive and all that, Stinky, but you overlooked something. This would be a lot more impressive if I was actually here, but I'm not." As she finished speaking Seline dissolved in a puff of smoke. There was a long wail of protest from the cavern below.

Outside on the hillside, Seline sat in the warm sun. "I can't believe he thought that would work. I can jump from parallel universe to universe for pity sake. Did he honestly think he could trap my physical body and starve me to death? Seriously?

"Moragah?"

"I am here, Seline."

"You ready to come home now?"

"That depends on you, my sister."

Seline morphed back into Shadow. "What now?"

"Shadow, I have severed much of the dark's ability to monitor me. It is safe for me to return, but I will do that only if you will fully accept who you are, what you are. The sisters will continue to pray to you, and you will need to answer those prayers. You will need to be there for them."

"I have been. Might I remind you just who was there for them and who ran away?"

"Moragah chuckled and sent her a wave of loving energy. "Point taken, my sister. So, what's your answer?"

"Fine, but you have to stop pussyfooting around and tell me all of it."

Another wave of warm loving energy swept through Lady Shadow bringing a smile to her face. "Yes, my sister. I'll tell you all of it. When Mai was killed and Tasha nearly so as well, I realized I just wasn't equipped to do what needed to be done. When I first came to this world, I had the necessary powers, but I was defeated and destroyed by the dark anyway.

"Once Penny awakened me, I tried to pick up and start over, using the same methods I had always relied on. It wasn't working. In desperation I sought a way to thwart the dark, and by happy chance I heard a woman's prayer for help.

"When I enhanced you, my sister, I gave you everything, access to all of it, all the power of creation I had at my disposal I gave to you. You didn't disappoint, Seline. I'm as proud of you as I could possibly be.

"You aren't bound to this planet or this time, or even this plane of existence. You aren't confined by any rules that bind me or my compatriots. You and you alone have full freedom, what you do with that is up to you. Seline, you are now the true power in this game of light versus dark. What will you do now?"

"I'll do as I swore to my goddess I would do, push back the dark, re-establish the balance. Just as you are the goddess of wisdom, defender of the weak, I will be the goddess of balance, and strive to maintain that balance so every human will have the ability to choose between them. Their soul journey is not mine to choose or interfere with."

Lady Shadow felt the great wave of relief that swept through Moragah. "That's what you were hoping for, wasn't it?"

"Yes, my sister, it was."

"I see it now. By accepting the title of Defender of the Weak, you put yourself in a weakened position. Why did you do that?"

"The very first priestess I created so long ago gave me that title, and I loved her beyond reasoning, so I embraced it. Penny will never know how much she reminds me of Alea.

"So, Sister Shadow, I will return with you, but I'll remain the defender of the weak, a healer goddess, and I'll hold back from the battles and confrontations with the forces of the dark. That task I leave to you, for you are far better equipped for it. You are my equal now and more, Shadow, and my ally. Only together can we accomplish what we must, restore the balance."

Lady Shadow neither spoke nor moved for several moments. Finally she rose to her feet. "Accepted. Let us return to our people, they're lost without you. Come." She waved her arm and disappeared from the hillside.

Lady Shadow reappeared in the living room of the mansion. All the daughters of Moragah were there, Ellen had called a meeting. "Welcome back." Ellen smiled as she kissed Lady Shadow's cheek. "Did you find Moragah?"

"I did. She will return to us."

"She will? When?" asked Penny as she leaped to her feet.

"Now," came the voice of Moragah as the vast presence filled them all with sweet loving energy. There were sighs of relief and cries of joy all round. "Be at peace, my daughters, for I will never abandon you again. I beg forgiveness, but it was necessary."

"Can you tell us why?" asked Penny.

"Yes, dear Penny, I will tell why I did what I did. I realized that what had happened to my people so long ago was about to happen again, but this time I was prepared, for I had in place someone who could prevent the dark and save my children.

"My sister Shadow was reluctant to accept her power, her true place in the universe. By abdicating my position as your guardian, I forced her to rise to the occasion. Now, my daughters, may I present to you the Lady Shadow, Goddess of Balance. It is she who will lead you in the struggle to push back the dark. I will remain as a healer goddess, defender of the weak. I'm sorry to have put you through that, but it was necessary to save you, for I could not do it myself.

"I'm so thrilled with all of you and delighted to be reunited with you."

With that the vast presence pulled back but remained close and they all could feel her. Shadow looked at all the smiling faces and sighed. Ryder grinned at her. "You gotta turn it up just a bit."

"What? What are you talking about?" asked Shadow as she morphed into Seline.

"Your energy, my goddess," replied Ryder. "I'm thrilled to have Moragah's energy back surrounding me, but I can still feel you too. I just want you to turn it up a bit so the two balance. That's what you're supposed to do, right? Keep the balance?"

Seline laughed with delight. "Okay, Ryder, how's this?"

Ryder cocked her head as though listening, then grinned anew. "Yeah, that's way better. Now I've got both of you. It's like floating on happy. So, what's our next move, Lady Shadow?"

"Now we consolidate our position, make safe our two cities. With luck we can lower the shields soon."

"Lower the shields?"

"Yes, Penny, lower the shields. If we don't the dark wins while we cower behind invisible walls, besides, I think we're a bit short handed. In truth, I probably should have taken the mansion to Georgia City, kept all our forces together. Ah well, too late now.

"Yes, the shields. Without enough personnel we can't man them and police a whole city at the same time. I'd like to drop the shields so our people can cross the border and back unhindered. I'm sure Miranda can spot any trouble before it manifests, and I promise I'll be less than gentle dealing with it.

"Speaking of dealing with it, I've made a deal with the Kaufman brothers. They'll tell me all they know of the Brotherhood, and I'll return them to Earth."

"You're just going to let them walk?"

"Yes, Tasha, my fierce sister, I am. However, I doubt that you'll be willing to extend them the same courtesy."

"I'm not following you."

"I promised to return them to Earth in exchange for the information. I didn't promise to protect them once they got here. I'll take them to their home, but I want you there when we arrive. Once I have what I need, they're all yours.

"So, tomorrow we lower our shields and see how it goes. If all is well then Tasha and I will deal with the Kaufman brothers. From there I'll continue to dismantle the Brotherhood until I'm satisfied it will no longer be a threat.

"While I do that, you ladies begin making plans to return the cities to the humans as soon as it's convenient."

"Return it to the humans?" asked Penny.

"Starting to like your job?"

Lady Blue laughed at that. "No, girl, I'll be more than happy to hand it off, but what's the long-term plan?"

"The plan is to let the humans govern themselves, but we will retain a visible presence. We will maintain the shields, patrol the mean streets, etc."

"Oh yeah, I'm liking that plan," grinned Lacy. "So, today we kick back?"

"Yes my sisters, today we kick back and luxuriate in Moragah's return to us."

Justice

In the end they gave it three more days before they lowered the shields, and Shadow stayed close for two more. Finally, she was ready to deal with the two billionaires who'd tried so hard to kill her and take over the country. The day was well along when she appeared in the Georgia City headquarters.

"Greetings, Lady Shadow."

"Good to see you Intel. Is Tasha near?"

"Right here, boss," came a cheerful voice behind her. "Are we doing the nasty tonight?"

"We are. Are you ready?"

Tasha went cold instantly. "Oh yeah, I'm more than ready to deal with those two bastards. Let's do it."

Shadow reached for her hand then they disappeared. They reappeared inside a mansion. They could hear servants in the distance, but the ornate office was quiet with an air of having been unused for some time.

"Hide yourself, Tasha. I'll bring them here, get the information as promised, then you can have them. You will dispense justice for the lives lost, and I will be witness for you. Are you ready?"

"Ready, go get 'em."

Lady Shadow vanished, and Lady Justice melted into the dimness of the room. She felt no trepidation or regret for what she would soon do, but she did feel some satisfaction that Justice would soon be delivered.

THE SUN WAS HOT, BUT the two men were quite comfortable under the spreading trees. The conversation was still going on. "Brother, is it truly so bad here? The climate's warm, there's food in plenty."

"It's still a prison, Stanton, solitary confinement no less. Wouldn't you enjoy a hot shower, a shave, getting into a decent suit, having servants prepare your food. A glass of fine whiskey, Stanton, surely you must miss that."

"I miss all of it, David; the problem is the Brotherhood. Even if she doesn't kill us, they will."

"No, she'll eliminate them, have no fear of that."

"But she wants the names of the top men in the brotherhood. We don't know who that is. We can't give her what she needs."

"We can give her plenty to keep her and the Brotherhood busy for months. She'll finish off the ones we give her, probably bring them here until they crack, then they'll give her more. She'll work her way to the top, finish the lot of them, and then we'll be free.

"While she's busy doing that we can rebuild our power base in the senate, regain control of ... look, there she is now. Come on, let's get out of here." Both men rose and hurried toward the Elvish warrior who sat atop a dragon.

As they near she climbed down to the ground and stepped to meet them. "Gentlemen, I have returned for your answer. Are you ready to give me all you know of the Brotherhood in exchange for a return to Earth?"

"We are," replied David Kaufman. "May I ask where on Earth you will take us?"

"I assumed you would wish to return to a familiar place. Would the office in your mansion be acceptable to you?"

"That would be more than acceptable, Lady Shadow."

"Then we go. Aeroth, return home now, dear friend, rest and await my call." The dragon snorted at the two men then stepped into the shadows beneath the trees and disappeared. "Gentlemen, touch my robe."

They each took hold of her sleeve then the universe seemed to wink out. They came to themselves, gasping for breath, but in David's office in the mansion. "Now, gentlemen, if you would be so kind. Take pen and paper, make me a list of everyone you know in the Brotherhood who is above you in rank. I will also need to know where to find them."

"We don't know their constant whereabouts ..."

"A general address will be sufficient. Quickly now, daylight is fading and so is my patience."

"Just a few minutes more," said David as he hurriedly wrote. At length he finished and handed her two sheets of paper with a list of names and addresses. "That's all we're aware of."

"Is any one of these the top man for the organization?"

"No, I'm afraid not. I did tell you that before, however, some of those I have named will surely be able to point you in the right direction."

"Indeed so. Very well then, you have fulfilled your part of the bargain. Are you satisfied I have fulfilled mine?"

"Yes."

"Then our business is satisfactorily concluded. I bid you adieu gentlemen. They're all yours Justice."

"Justice?"

"Oh god, David, look." He looked where his brother pointed. There was a vague figure of a woman over against the far wall. She stepped into the last rays of sunshine, her dark skin glowing in the light, a curtain of raven hair hiding most of her face, and a smile that did not reach her eyes. Those eyes were so cold, both men shivered and stepped back as she moved toward them.

"Who are you?" stammered one of the brothers.

"I am Justice, and I've come for you both. Each of you has organized an attack on our cities, our people, and our sisters, resulting in the loss of hundreds of innocent lives. For these crimes of premeditated murder, you will now face Justice."

"No, no, that wasn't part of the deal, Shadow."

"You agreed that our deal had been satisfactorily concluded," said Shadow. "This no longer has anything to do with me."

"But we gave you ..." He got no further as the young beauty moved and was suddenly behind him, her arms encircling his neck. A quick twist and he went limp in her arms. She tossed the body aside.

Stanton Kaufman ran to the door, but it wouldn't open. He turned back, trembling in fear. "No, please, Lady Shadow, please, put me back on the planet, please."

"That decision is not mine to make. Lady Justice, will you grant this man clemency, substitute exile for death?"

He began to weep as he saw his death in those cold eyes. "No. The hundreds of dead homeless people of Georgia City weren't given the option of a lifelong vacation. No, you pay for your crimes."

A single wail of fear and protest escaped his lips as she seized him up and wrapped those unforgiving arms around his neck. A quick twist and he went limp. She dropped him to the floor. "Justice is served."

Lady Shadow reached for her hand. "Come, sister, let us be away from here." Tasha took her hand and they vanished from the room.

TASHA LOOKED AROUND, puzzled, as they reappeared. "Quite a view, isn't it?"

"Lady Shadow, why are we half way up a mountain instead of back at headquarters?"

"I think we should talk."

Tasha chuckled at that. "I'm all yours, girl. What's on your mind?"

"Tasha, I don't think I'm the only one who's been holding back a bit. Both you and Kara are as guilty as I am."

Tasha sighed and relaxed back against the boulder behind her. "I scare myself, Seline, I go so cold, no compassion at all, nothing. I'm afraid to let myself go in case I won't be able to make it back. I know Kara feels the same way. She's afraid to let the Fallen Angel out for fear she might not be able to get back from it. That persona draws power from a dark place, so does Justice."

"I do understand, Tasha, been there. I hear you."

"But?"

"But we're neutrals, we're not lightworkers, we draw from both powers. For healing and making things right and fair, we draw on the light, but when we go in to battle we're going to have to draw on our full strength, that means both dark and light energy.

"Tasha, when Mai got killed and you nearly didn't make it, Moragah threw caution to the wind, took a leap of faith, and made me. After that she made the people I'd need to get the job done, a super seeker, a visionary, and a super warrior."

"Okay."

"She also souped up your abilities when she healed you from the wounds you took. However, you've held back from using them."

"How did you know?"

"In the battle of the fishmen, I saw you fighting. Tasha, you'd give Lacy a hard time if you let go."

"Okay, so, why are we having this conversation?"

"I recognized one of the names Kaufman gave me. The man rules a small country in South America. That country is heavily militarized, and I believe it to be a stronghold of the Brotherhood, probably where that gang we fought is located. I expect to have to go after them and I want you, the Warrior, and the original Fallen Angel with me."

"Shadow?"

"Penny is a true defender, that will be no place for her. Lenora and Ryder are more hunter than warrior, and I will not risk Miranda. I'll need you and Kara to go in at full strength."

"That'll be a hard sell with Kara."

"I know."

"There's more, isn't there?"

"Yes. Tasha, I want to do something to make you a hundred times more effective. Will you permit me to enhance you even more?"

"Are you serious?"

"Completely."

"Have you ever done this before?"

"No."

"Will it hurt?"

"Probably."

"You're not reassuring me, Seline." Shadow chuckled at that. "What do you want to do?"

"Tasha, now you can step against a wall and seemingly disappear. I want to take that a bit further. I want you to be able to hide there as before if that is your desire. However, if you wish to be in another place, I want to make that possible for you. I also want to make it so you can take another with you and teleport to any place you might wish. In effect, you would no longer need the portal device."

"Is this necessary? The portal device works pretty well."

Shadow grinned at that. "Why is that, do you think?"

"Seline, what did you do?"

"Well, the portals should only be able to take you from one point to another, but I've seen you and Lenora doing all sorts of interesting things with them. It shouldn't take much for this to work. Come on, trust me, it'll be fun."

She was grinning, and Tasha laughed. "All right, my goddess, I'll trust you, do it." Before she could brace herself she felt a tingle in her head then a sharp pain that was there and gone. "Ow, crap."

Shadow gathered the girl into her arms and sent a wave of healing energy through her. "Moragah, did I get it right?"

"You did, Seline. I'm quite proud of you for that one," came the voice of their goddess.

Shadow stood and offered her hand to Tasha. "Time to test it out, girl."

"How's it supposed to work?"

"Just think of where you want to be then fade into it like you do to hide in the shadows." Tasha nodded, took Shadow's hand then they disappeared from the mountainside. They reappeared at headquarters, right beside Intel, startling him.

"Jesus, J, what the hell?" She just laughed and hugged him.

"That worked well, Lady Justice. Speak with Kara and prepare, I wish to leave on the morrow." With that she vanished.

"Speak with Kara about what?" asked Kara.

"I'm sorry honey, but Shadow's going to ask you to do something you don't want to do."

"And that is?"

"She's going after the Brotherhood's stronghold. She wants me, the Warrior, and the Angel with her."

"Oh no, I ..."

"Kara, she won't force you, but if you agree to go, she'll need you at full power, she'll need the Fallen Angel."

Kara stood looking into her eyes for a long moment. "Are you going?"

"Yes. Honey, Seline enhanced me with a special ability, and I know why she did it."

"What did she do?"

Tasha took her hand and grinned. "Hang onto your hat." An instant later they were outside the mansion in North Bay. Kara had only a moment to gaze around when Tasha blinked, and they were back where they started.

"Holy crap. Wow, teleportation, that's a handy talent. Why did she give you this, do you think?"

"So if it all goes to hell sideways, I'll be able to get you to safety. Sweetheart, I won't ask you to do this if you don't think you can let the Angel out."

"But you'll go anyway."

"Yes."

Kara gazed into those deep brown eyes that she loved so much. She swallowed hard then spoke. "All right, I'll go. Tash, I'll need a few beers and a couple of hours to get in the right headspace. You might not like who comes out of that room."

"Silly woman, I'll love you no matter who you are. Let's get some rest then get up early and put you in a nasty mood."

"Okay, but I want some cuddles before I turn into the bitch from hell."

In the Lion's Den

It was early, just before dawn, when Tasha awakened. She lightly kissed Kara's forehead then slipped from the room. Returning, she set a six pack of beer on the bedside table then left again, closing the door behind her.

Out in the main office, Intel was already at work. "Lady J, did I see you going with a six of beer?"

"Yeah, it was for Kara."

"What's going on, Tasha?"

"We're going out with Shadow today, taking down the Brotherhood's stronghold. This is going to be nasty and Shadow wants Kara at full strength."

"Okay, so what does that mean?"

"That means the strongest of us, next to Shadow herself, will walk out of that bedroom, and she'll be in a nasty mood. For the love of god, do not irritate her."

"What aren't you telling me, J?"

"Kara is the original Fallen Angel."

"The orig ... sweet baby Jesus, you mean ..."

"I do. She keeps that locked away inside her all the time because the Angel feeds on rage, rage at what was done to her. Right now she's having beer for breakfast and reviewing things she'd rather forget.

"Shit, I just felt her shut Moragah out. She's almost ready."

At that point Kara closed the bedroom door with a bang. She entered the room dressed in her motorcycle leathers with the Chosen colors on the back. "Hey there," said Tasha, "want something real to eat before we head out?"

"I already had breakfast. Let's just get this shit over with."

Intel swallowed hard and stepped away from her, then he noticed Tasha's eyes. He'd never seen her so cold. She reached for Kara's hand. "Let's go." As Kara gripped her hand they disappeared.

They rematerialized in the living room of the mansion. Several people were there having coffee. Penny took one look at Kara and set her mug down. "Oh shit."

"Hey Sis."

"Hi Angel, something up?"

"Yeah, it is. Today is payback day."

"Payback day?"

"The Brotherhood," said Seline as she set down her coffee and morphed into Lady Shadow. "We're going into their main stronghold. These men control much of the world's crime, drugs and slavery. It is from this place the gangs came to help the fishmen."

"All right, I'm up for it."

"No, Penny, you're not coming," said Kara.

"Excuse me?"

"Listen you, you're a defender, a woman of compassion, the one who dug me out of my own personal hell. This is going to be nasty, no place for you, no place for anybody who might hesitate or hold back. Besides, I may need you to help me get back.

"Ah, fuck it, are we going or are we having a tea party?"

"We're going," said Shadow. "Lacy, with me."

Lacy gave Miranda a quick peck on the cheek then stepped up beside Shadow. Miranda looked distraught as they all vanished from the room.

"Ellen, what's going on?" asked Penny.

"They're going after the heart of the Brotherhood," sighed Ellen. "They'll be facing a lot of fairly modern military, hundreds of members of that murderous gang, plus god knows what. Shadow took her best warriors with her, but she left the truest heart of the sisters behind.

"She left you, Penny to take her place if she doesn't make it back. You've always been the big sister to the others. She left Lenora for her sense of justice, right and wrong, and she left Miranda to keep her safe."

"Bugger that," declared Miranda. "We need to be there with her. I'll find her. Who does she think she's playing with here ...."?

"No, Miranda, my child," came the voice of Moragah as the vast presence of the goddess engulfed them. "You must remain here, even I must remain behind."

"You, Moragah? Why? What's going on? Seline's a goddess, she could take all those guys by herself. Why did she need the others?"

"Shadow needs the warriors to keep the humans at bay while she deals with the true enemy."

Miranda gulped and went pale. "The god of darkness."

"Yes. That one will surely be there to aid its minions."

"All the more reason for us to be there," said Penny.

"No, dear Penny. Shadow would not leave the world unprotected. She left behind those who could defend the weak if she isn't able to. No, we will remain here and worry while our goddess goes into battle."

"Our goddess, Moragah?"

"Caught that, did you, Penny. How I do love that sharp mind of yours. Yes, our goddess. Both the light and the dark fear the other, and so they hold back, retaining the power for themselves. I did the same, and it cost me, for I was defeated, left alone and bereft.

"You awaken me, dear Penny, and so, together, we set out upon the quest for balance. Sadly, I realized I was losing once again, and so I made Shadow. I looked into her soul and saw the sweetness there, but the strength as well, and I gambled all.

"I didn't tell her, dared not tell her, what I had done, but I was desperate. When I made Shadow I gave her everything, full access to the light and dark, full access to total universal creation.

"Our Lady Shadow is greater than us all, she is limitless, unbeatable, unstoppable, omnipotent. There is really only one thing for her to fear."

"Herself," breathed Penny.

"Yes, Penny, that is the true battle Shadow fights this day."

"And the others? Them as well?"

"Yes. I see your fear for Kara, so know this. Shadow enhanced Tasha with teleportation so she could bring Kara out if necessary."

"Yeah, okay, cool, but I hate being left out of the action."

"Not me," sighed Lenora as she sat back down. "I'm content to let the true warriors fight the big battles. Come on, kids, we have to sit this one out. Come on back here and worry with me."

Nodding their agreement, they returned to their seats, but didn't speak. Moragah sent them waves of loving, comforting energy, but they still worried.

THE WARRIORS APPEARED on a hillside overlooking a heavily armed compound in a small valley below. "This the place?" asked Kara.

"It is," replied Shadow. "By the looks of the heavy military presence, we are expected."

"How could they know?" asked Lacy.

"If it were us, I'd say Miranda saw it coming, but these men fear the visionaries. The Brotherhood probably have visual surveillance on all their people," replied Shadow.

"You think they were watching the Kaufmans' office?" asked Tasha.

"Probably, and since the Kaufman brothers gave me a list, and this place was known to them, they're waiting for us."

"Lady Shadow, if they knew we were coming, do you think the big shots are still here?"

"No, Tasha, I'm sure the top men have made their escape already. Killing them is not our purpose here."

"No? Care to share?"

"Our task is to push back the darkness, not defeat it. We seek to restore the balance between the light and dark. If we destroy this place, and whatever men they have left to take the fall, we deliver them a serious blow, push them back."

"Forgive me, but why not defeat it, the dark, I mean?" asked Lacy. "I just don't get it, Boss."

"Lacy, my savage warrior sister, there needs to be a balance of energies, influences, in the world. Each human's soul is on a journey of self-discovery, of growth. Each soul must have free choice in its travels on that path.

"They must decide for themselves which path to take in this lifetime, light or dark. We cannot make that choice for them. To utterly defeat the dark would also destroy the world as surely as it would to allow the dark free reign. No, there must be a balance, and it's up to we neutrals to maintain that balance.

"That's why we're here today, to restore the balance. The lord of the darkness is here as well to aid his creations. It is he I must face, and you must entertain the rest while I do."

"Then let's stop fucking around and get it done," growled Kara. "Tasha, see the way they're all bunched up in that courtyard, just behind the tank?"

"Yeah?"

"Drop us in there and let's get this show on the road."

"You got it, sweetheart." Tasha grabbed Kara and Lacy by the hand, and they vanished from the hillside to re-appear right beside the tank, in the midst of dozens of soldiers.

Someone shouted the alarm and Kara hurled him against the side of the tank, killing him instantly. She popped up her armor and went at them, guns blazing. Lacy had already downed over a dozen men by that time, and Tasha had accounted for several more.

Bullets were flying everywhere, and without the magic armor they surely would have been killed. Protected by the alien armor, they moved through the courtyard like semi invisible ghosts. It took a while, but the area was eventually cleared. Now they were down to the few who'd managed to take cover and hide.

They stopped to confer for a moment but had no chance. As soon as they slowed down and became visible, a door flew open and fresh troops charged in, guns chattering a song of death. With a snarl of rage, Kara tore into them, Lacy right at her side, and Tasha a heartbeat behind. These new troops were more disciplined, and they didn't have the disadvantage of being taken by surprise.

In spite of their great strength and speed, they were only three against hundreds. Slowly but surely they got pushed back until they were nearly crushed against the wall. Heavy steel nets began to fall on them and they were further hampered. The constant pounding of the bullets was taking a toll, and it was looking bad.

Tasha grabbed both Kara and Lacy by the arm and they vanished. They reappeared behind the soldiers and renewed their attack. Both Kara and Lacy were using knives now, but Tasha had retrieved a gun from a downed soldier. The battle continued.

They fought into the middle of the soldiers, taking a terrible toll, but once again they were getting bogged down. Several men had grabbed onto Lacy and were dragging her down, Tasha the same.

With a scream of pure hate Kara tore into them and Tasha was back on her feet. Together they ripped the men off Lacy then Tasha transported them back to the hillside. Still screaming her battle challenge, Kara spun to Tasha, then shook herself to get hold of the rage before she spoke.

"Tasha, what the hell?"

"We're getting our asses kicked, there's just too many of them."

"Fuck that shit. Put me back in there."

"No, Kara honey."

"I mean it, Tash, put me back, right in the middle of them. Lacy, you stay here. Tasha, drop me in then get the hell out of there."

"What're you going to do?"

"I'm going to cut loose on these fuckers, that's what I'm going to do." She turned and shouted down at the courtyard below. "You bastards hear me. The angel is coming for you and you're going straight to hell. Do it Tasha."

Tasha grabbed her arm and they vanished to reappear in the midst of hundreds of heavily armed soldiers. Tasha vanished again, and Kara burst into flame. *"Stand still!"* All the soldiers froze in place.

Back on the hillside Lacy and Tasha heard that scream of pure rage and watched in horror as the courtyard erupted in flames. It burned. It burned so hot the concrete walls were melted, the ground boiled up, and lava flowed from the gateway.

Tasha swallowed hard and started to weep. Nothing could have survived that, nothing. Suddenly Lacy grabbed her arm. "Holy shit. Tasha look, there, look. Is that ...?"

"Kara!" Tasha appeared beside the small figure and gathered it into her arms. They re-appeared beside Lacy and Kara sank to the ground with a sigh.

"Hi guys, either of you got any beer?"

"Sorry, Angel, we drank the last of it while you were playing with fire," grinned Lacy. "Gotta tell you, girl, you're one hell of a fighter, but that fire thing really rocks."

"Yeah, well, I don't like to use it unless I have to, but these bastards deserved it. I wonder how Shadow's making out?"

"I just hope you didn't cook her," sighed Tasha.

"Seline knows I use fire, Tash honey. She specifically asked for the angel, she knew there'd be fire. She'd be ready for it."

"Yeah, I guess. Honey, are you okay?"

"I'm good. Lacy, you see any reinforcements coming for those guys?"

"There's something coming up the road, not sure what ... yeah, more of them. You catch your breath, I'll get this bunch."

"Knock yourself out," grinned Kara.

"Tasha, can I get a lift down the hill?"

With a laugh, Lady Justice took Lacy's arm and transported her to the road right in front of the oncoming trucks. She left her there and returned to Kara. The angel was back on her feet and gazing down the road beyond where Lacy was taking apart the two truckloads of soldiers. "Looks like more coming, my turn next."

"You mean our turn next."

"Stay out of it Tasha, this is personal."

Tasha grabbed her arm and spun her around then went nose to nose with her. "Listen, Fallen Angel, don't give me that crap. I'm your wife, I love you, all of you. If Kara wants to cuddle in the moonlight, we cuddle. If the angel goes to war, I go to war at her side. Got that?"

Suddenly Kara grinned, and with a twinkle in her eye, kissed Tasha on the nose. "Damn you're sexy when you get all fierce on me."

"Dammit, Kara."

"Look, there's no justice about what I'm doing here, nothing fair. I'm just killing the bastards that work for the fuckers who ran the operation that held me slave."

"I don't care, we go together."

"Okay, if you're sure. It looks like Lacy's stopped for a beer with company coming. Let's go."

"Together."

"Yes, together. Come on or Lacy'll have all the fun."

They appeared beside Lacy. "More coming?" she asked.

"More coming," replied Kara. "Tasha gave me stress, said I have to share. Pisses me off, but what can you do? All together then?"

"I get that, Miranda henpecks me too. Sure, all together. Let's go." Tasha was still shaking a finger at them both as the enemy arrived and opened fire.

Slowly, but surely, they defeated the soldiers then moved further down the road to intercept the next group. Suddenly Warrior started to swear. She'd spotted the war planes. "Fuck. Tasha, get us out of here."

They reappeared on the hillside as missile after missile slammed into the compound and mansion. Silently they watched as the rubble settled, then they saw the dome shining in the destroyed mansion at the center of the compound.

Tasha began to cheer. "Yes, she was ready for that, you bastards." She yelped and stepped back as a gout of hellfire erupted from beside her to engulf one of the warplanes, exploding it. Kara stepped forward, screamed a challenge of rage and hate as she sent the fire against the second plane.

The second plane exploded, and Kara sank to the ground with a sigh. "I'm going to sleep for a week when this is over."

"Sweet Jesus, Kara," breathed Lacy. "Why the hell did Moragah want me when she already had you? I'm not in your class, girl."

"The hell you're not, Lacy. Besides, Moragah didn't have me. Kara is Moragah's baby, little miss goody two shoes, defender of the weak. I'm the fallen angel, I draw my power from the darkness. I'm running hot today because the lord of the dark is here and I'm pulling power from him. Moragah doesn't want anything to do with this shit."

"She's still inside you, sis."

"No she's not. I shut her out before we came here. Right now I'm a true child of the dark. What most people don't understand about the dark is its desire to control or destroy everything, including itself.

"I know, perverse shit, but there it is. Christ, I hope that was the last of them, I'm beat to a snot."

Lacy nodded. "Go ahead, Angel, catch a nap. I'll wake you if the fun starts again."

"Thanks, sis, but I'll stay awake until Shadow gets back."

"Damn good idea," said Tasha. "Incoming choppers."

"Ah for fuck sake," growled Kara as she rose to her feet. "Where?"

Three attack helicopters came in out of the sun, but they went straight to the compound. There was nothing there for them to attack. The three warriors watched as the machines found and investigated the dead and destroyed trucks on the roadway. As they hovered over one truck three warriors appeared beneath them.

Lacy hurled a stone and knocked one of the gunners out of the chopper. As he fell Tasha opened fire on the machine. It swung around to attack her, but Lacy had leaped high and caught hold on the open doorway. The men shot and kicked at her, but all to no avail. Soon the machine spun out of control and plunged toward the ground. The Warrior jumped out just before it crashed.

Lacy landed and easily rolled back to her feet to see Kara and Tasha walk out of a wall of flame. The other chopper was down, the third one fled. Lady Justice transported them back to the hill top once again.

LADY SHADOW APPEARED in the entryway of the mansion. The sounds of battle from outside were easily heard, and bullets tore through the heavy doors. The projectiles fell harmlessly from her armor as she walked deeper into the building, her head turning one way then another as she sought for the hidden rooms, the safe places for the leaders to hide.

A deep sinister voice broke through her concentration. "Why aren't you outside saving your sisters? You know they're being tortured, you can hear the screams. Go to them, Shadow. You can save them, you can."

Shadow wondered, what was it about the voice of darkness that made her want to taunt it in Seline's voice. "Seriously Stinky? You're trying to use illusion on *me*? Is that the best you've got?"

She continued on, but the illusions continued to batter at her. She heard the screams of torment from her warriors but ignored it. Ellen's face appeared, and she watched as Ellen was ravaged, heard her screams for help, but she saw through the illusion and ignored it.

The door to the safe room was before her, but so was that illusion of Ellen, or was it illusion? Shadow felt something drip onto her hand. She looked down, it was blood, Ellen's blood. David Kaufman was holding the knife he'd driven through Ellen's side. With a grin of pure delight, he passed it to Shadow.

She let the knife fall into her hand, felt it's weight, the sharpness of the blade, slick with the blood of her lover. It felt real, Ellen's cold dead eyes staring at her looked real, and Kaufman's gloating laughter sounded real. Deep inside her a murderous rage began to burn.

"Yes, my beloved," oozed the voice from the darkness, "come to me, embrace me. Come to me, my loving bride, and together we will erase these scum from the face of the Earth. Side by side we will prevail against all who stand before us. Come to me now, together we will avenge Ellen."

Shadow swallowed hard, trembling with the power of the rage inside her. Just as she was about to reach for that dark hand, a small dragon walked across her field of vision. It stopped to gaze at her with sad eyes, then turned its back and lay down.

The voice of the dark kept at her, the illusions of Ellen increased, but Shadow's entire focus was channeled into remembering the dragon's name. Something inside her, more powerful than the rage, needed to remember the name of the dragon. From outside there came a scream of primal rage as Kara reached for the darkness within her. The room began to heat up, the illusion flickered, and the name came to her tongue.

"Aeroth." A bugle of delight came from the dragon as it leaped to its feet, increasing in size, and enfolding Shadow within it's wings, sheltering her from the terrifying heat. Beneath the wings of the dragon, Lady Shadow dispelled the illusions of the dark, shattering them and casting them aside.

She created a bubble of defense against the heat and melting stone then turned and opened the door to the safe room. Three men cowered there. The darkness battered at her as she stepped inside, the dragon at her side. A wave of her hand and, with a scream of impotent rage, the darkness was cast out, unable to reach her.

The three men howled as though in pain as their guardian was pushed aside. It continued to attack Shadow, but she ignored it. She realized her mistake, by responding in Seline's voice she had acknowledged the dark and thus, granted it power to reach her. She smiled gently as she hugged the dragon's neck. "Thank you, dear friend. I'm all right now, return to your rest."

"Are you certain?" asked a soft voice in her mind.

"I am."

"Should I go to the sister of dragons?"

"Not yet, but she will need you in the end. Keep an eye on her for me?"

"I will." With that the dragon faded into the shadows of the room.

Lady Shadow turned to the three men cowering behind an overturned table. A wave of her hand and the table exploded into splinters, exposing them to her view. With a scream one man opened fire with the automatic weapon in his hands. She ignored it.

With swift strides she crossed the room and drove a shining sword through the man's body. A spinning kick crushed the skull of another. The third lay on the floor, whimpering. She seized him by the collar and lifted him into the air.

"Be still now and I will take you to a place of safety."

It took a while for her words to penetrate his terrified mind. "What? What did you say?"

She set him back on his feet. "I said I'd take you to a place of safety, but first, tell me the names of the men you answer to."

"The men I ...?

"In the Brotherhood, who are your superiors? Name them."

"They lay dead before you, dead by your own hand. I know of no other by name." Her eyes darkened and he began to tremble. "That one," he babbled, pointing to one of the dead men on the floor. "His phone will have a special number, known only as master Ex. He is their superior. Please."

Shadow bent and retrieved the phone from the man's pocket and passed it to her captive. "Call him." With trembling hands he did as she bade him, then passed it back to her as it rang.

"Is it done?" asked a voice.

"Yes, it is done," she replied. "You failed again. This is Shadow. Hear me well, disband the Brotherhood or I will hunt you all to the death." She crushed the phone in her hand. "And now for you, come." She took him by the collar and they vanished then reappeared beside the three tired warriors on the hillside.

"There you are, took you long enough," groused Kara.

"I missed you too, sweet sister," grinned Shadow. "Look closely," she said as she held the man out towards the devastation below. "Mark well the destroyed compound, the dead and dying soldiers, empty weapons, burned out trucks, and destroyed aircraft. This was all done by my warriors, just the three of them.

"Tasha, take them back to the mansion, I'll be right there."

"Yes, my goddess," sighed Tasha as she reached for Kara and Lacy.

They disappeared, and she turned to the captive. "I will leave you here to attest to what has happened. Know this and tell the rest. I will hunt the Brotherhood into extinction." With that, she too disappeared.

THE THREE WARRIORS reappeared in the living room of the mansion to the shrieks of joy from those still gathered there. Moragah came and enfolded them in a wave of loving healing energy. Cradled in the loving embrace of the mother goddess, they began to relax.

"See, I told you they were about finished," grinned Miranda as she took Lacy in her arms. "Come sit down, sweetheart, I'll bring you something to eat."

Tasha guided Kara into a chair then collapsed down beside her. Shadow appeared and morphed into Seline, then fell into Ellen's arms. Tasha took out her phone and sent Intel a text. "We're back. Success. Everybody Ok."

"Well?" asked Ellen as Miranda returned with a tray of high energy snacks and several bottles of water. She started handing out the water as Seline began her report.

"We found the place, no problem. The angel was spoiling for a fight by then, so the three amigos went at them. Dear lord, I'm so impressed. My sisters, you rock, and I'm so proud of you I could split.

"While they kept the ground troops busy, I went after the bosses. I managed to find their safe room, but the voice of darkness stopped me. In the beginning he tried illusion, but that didn't work, at least not at first. I am, after all, a master of illusion.

"However, I made a serious mistake. I responded to the illusion with sarcasm, that created a connection for him. The next thing I knew I was in a torture chamber, watching the Kaufman brothers torture and murder Ellen."

Ellen's arms were instantly around her shoulders, cuddling her close. "It caught me by surprise, the power of it. It was real, so very real, and I was paralyzed. I have no idea at all how long I was rooted to the spot, staring at the mangled body of my lover. I don't know how long I was there, but I know time passed without me.

"I was slowly falling under the spell. Kaufman laughed as he passed me the knife he used to kill my beloved Ellen. I felt the sharp blade pierce my skin, the slickness of the blood, and I was ready to reach for the hand of darkness. His voice called to me, calling me his bride, urging me to join him in vengeance against the entire human race.

"The rage welled up in me and I was reaching out to that seductive voice when something so utterly unusual happened that it broke my focus. A small dragon walked across the room. It irritated me that I couldn't remember its name.

"I shifted my focus to the dragon and eventually was able to recall his name. As soon as I spoke the name the dark's hold on me wavered. I felt Kara reach deep into the heart of darkness and pull the fire from it. That broke the connection and Aeroth came to me, protected me beneath his wings as the fire burned.

"Feeding the angel the power she desired weakened the dark, and as badly as he wanted her to stop, he couldn't make it happen, she was too strong, her need too great, her demand too powerful even for him to resist, and the fire burned deep into the ground.

"When she stopped he was weakened and I was stronger as the dragon fed me his love, his strength, and I arose, renewed. The illusion persisted for a short while, but I ignored it, as I should have in the beginning. The dark fled from me then.

"The Brotherhood had left three men there. I killed two and left the third alive with a message for his superiors. I said I'd hunt them to extinction."

"So you're going to finish all of them?" asked Miranda.

"No, not unless they come at us again. There's no need. We've done what we set out to do."

"What we set out to do?"

"Restore the balance. Take a hard look, Lady Watcher. Tell me we haven't brought back the balance."

Miranda closed her eyes for a moment then refocused on Seline. "There are a few places of utter darkness still in the world, but there are places of pure light as well. Yes, my goddess, I believe you're right, you have restored the balance."

"We, Lady Watcher, we, the sisters of balance, the warriors of justice, together we have restored the balance. Moragah, my sister, what say you?"

Moragah sent a wave of healing energy through them all. "Yes, my sister, you have indeed done the impossible. You have restored the balance. I am so very proud of you all."

"Sweet," grinned Lacy. "So now what happens?"

Seline rose to her feet and smiled. "First I have one more task to perform. Angel, come to me."

"Aw crap, Shadow, you're not going to make me all soft and fuzzy again, are you?"

Seline morphed into Lady Shadow. "Come to me, my fierce sister. Hug me now." Kara rolled her eyed and stepped into Shadow's embrace. They both began to glow with a bright light.

Suddenly Aeroth was there beside them and they all heard the voice of the dragon in their minds. "Let go, sister of dragons. I will take you to our home where you can rest until needed again."

Kara nodded and hugged Shadow tighter. The dragon faded, and so did the light. With a shy smile Kara reached for Tasha's hand. "Okay, big sister, what did you do?"

Shadow smiled and patted her shoulder. "That part of you that is the Fallen Angel has gone to her rest in Dragonhome. There she will rest with the children of fire until you need her again. She will come if you call, but until then she will rest, and now so can you." She kissed Kara's cheek then morphed back into Seline who sat back with Ellen and snuggled into her arms.

IN THE DAYS AND WEEKS to follow Lenora returned to bounty hunting, bought a new house near where the old one had stood. The North Bay people set Morty back up in business and Mary-jo in a brand new B&B.

Miranda set her mother up in a nice apartment near the mansion where she was often a welcome visitor. Seline Elmore and Ellen were often seen in the city, as was Lady Shadow and the Viper.

Georgia City prospered under the rule of Lady Justice and Little Blue. Outside the cities Lady Blue and or the Warrior were occasionally seen in various parts of the country. All in all, life appeared to have returned to normal.

On a far off alien planet, Ryder and the Chosen settled in to their new clubhouse, aka the barracks on Eelion. Dex was especially pleased to have life return to his home planet after so long alone.

Over it all watched a lone rider on dragon back, ever watchful, every wary, and still reaching toward her potential.

The End

A nd now for a peek at something different. A number of years ago vampire stories were quite popular. When I jokingly suggested I might write one, a fan challenged me to actually do it, but to make it original, give it a fresh perspective. Always up for a challenge, I accepted. Immortal Tigress is the result. Take a look.

Immortal Tigress
By
Prudence MacLeod

Need

In the beginning there was need. She was only dimly aware of the world around her, a world filled with wonder, and yet fraught with danger. She was only aware of need, the need for food, for drink, safety from attack, fire for warmth and protection.

As she grew there came a new need, a need to mate, but that was not to be for she had grown too tall and strong too quickly, and thus she was shunned by the others. Eventually she became insistent and was driven away from the clan, for her sheer size and strength frightened them.

Alone and hungry, she sat beside a small tree near a stream, mourning, and trying to warm herself as she filled her empty belly with sweet grasses. Slowly she became aware of a fire in the sky. Gazing in wonder at the thing that grew steadily nearer, she was unaware of the danger stalking her. The fire from the sky hit the ground and exploded just as the great beast pounced. The beast tore at her body but was itself shredded by the exploding fireball.

Wounded and terrified, she lay beneath the body of the great cat, its life blood pouring out across her lips, while a strange glowing mist fell upon them. For a moment she drank greedily of the blood, then fainted away.

The body of the long toothed cat was still laying half across her when awareness returned, but the glowing mist was gone. The sun was up, and for some reason it disturbed her, and hurt her eyes. With a mighty heave she thrust the beast's carcass away and leaped to her feet, her wounds healed, and her great strength returned, redoubled. She wrenched a long fang with which to make a weapon, from the jaw of the cat. A moment later she found shelter from the sun among the trees. She would wait for darkness, and then she would hunt. She wanted, needed, the taste of the blood again. Now there was a stronger need than any she had ever known.

Murdered

"Vampire? Preposterous." John West met the eyes of all four of his friends and the stranger. "I don't believe a word of it."

"Please John, I know you think you love your wife, but do you really or is it just some compulsion she has laid on you?" The tall man began to sputter, but his friends hurried on. "John, how many times have you awakened to find your bed empty?"

"Ella often walks the gardens at night..."

"Yes she does," oozed the stranger in the room, a man with dark skin, cruel eyes, and a scar down the side of his face, wearing the garb of a priest. He'd said his name was Mobutu. "Don't you find that habit a bit odd, Mr. West?"

"Vampire. I just can't believe that my wife is a vampire." John West was visibly shaken and he was beginning to waver.

"Has she ever injured herself, Mr. West?" asked the priest. "If so, does she heal remarkably well? Do things that should damage the body seem to leave her unaffected? Has she aged in the fifteen years of your marriage?"

The harangue went on for hours and eventually they wore him down. John West sat, his head in his hands, shaking as he finally accepted what he was being told. "What am I going to do?"

The priest rose and passed him a vial. "This is laudanum, it will induce sleep; make certain she drinks it all. You must do this tonight before she goes for her walk. We shall be waiting for your signal. Once she's unconscious we'll come to you and deal with the rest."

"ELLA, I KNOW YOU PREFER to stay indoors during the day. Thank you so much for accompanying me."

"My skin burns too easily, Margaret, but it's a dark and cloudy day today, I'll be fine."

"Ella, what is it? You're sniffing the air like my husband's old hound."

"I thought I smelled something vile."

"Of course you did; we're not that far from London. Ah, here we are, Dr. Lawson's surgery. Just make yourself comfortable, Ella. I'm sure I won't be long."

The tall woman settled into a leather-bound chair to wait for her friend to be finished with the doctor. She tried reading, but couldn't focus on the print. Her mind wandered back over the years, thousands of years beyond anything a human could remember. She remembered the first time she had caught that scent. "Mobutu," she snarled as she ran that first meeting through her mind.

The world had been younger then and far from civilized. She had inadvertently created another like her, but not quite the same. She'd managed to gain control over the killing lust, but the other had not. Ella had stalked and killed it, later discovering that it had created more like itself, unable to control the killing lust. One by one she stalked and slew them all, all but one. Mobutu. He was the last.

She'd come upon him in a small clearing where he was tearing his victim apart slowly, trying to elicit more screams. An errant draft of wind had taken her scent to him just before she charged. He escaped. Snarling in rage at the miss, she dispatched the poor broken female he had been torturing. His scent was strong in her nostrils for she'd raked him down the face and his blood was on the ground.

She had stood snarling, testing the breeze for his scent when his voice drifted down to her from the cliff above. "I've escaped you, you murderous old hag," he'd shouted in a thick accent. "I will hunt you now. I am Mobutu; I will become your death."

Ella had hurled herself at the cliff face, but he was long gone by the time she reached the top. It was several hundred years before they met again.

Don't miss out!

Visit the website below and you can sign up to receive emails whenever Prudence MacLeod publishes a new book. There's no charge and no obligation.

https://books2read.com/r/B-A-ZKBBB-QPPTC

BOOKS 2 READ

Connecting independent readers to independent writers.

Also by Prudence MacLeod

Novan Witch
Assassin of Nova
Beyond Nova
Claimstake
Red Nova

Watch for more at https://www.prudencemacleod.com/.

Telling a story is like knitting a sweater. Start with a ball of possibilities, pull out one small thread and begin. With luck and patience you will create something quite wonderful.

About the Author

On a far off windswept island Jennifer Crandall sits with her dogs and cats creating fantastic stories for all to enjoy. She publishes as JL Crandall, Prudence MacLeod, and Jenni Leigh.

Read more at https://www.prudencemacleod.com/.